THE SURVIVALIST 3
THE QUEST

*The Survivalist series by Jerry Ahern,
published by New English Library*

THE SURVIVALIST 3
THE QUEST

Jerry Ahern

NEW ENGLISH LIBRARY

First published in the USA in 1981 by Kensington Publishing Corporation

Copyright © 1981 by Jerry Ahern

First NEL Paperback Edition November 1983
Reprinted November 1983
Reprinted February 1984
Reprinted November 1984

NEL Books are published by
New English Library,
Mill Road, Dunton Green,
Sevenoaks, Kent.
Editorial Office: 47 Bedford Square, London WC1B 3DP

Printed and bound in Great Britain by
Cox & Wyman Ltd, Reading

British Library C.I.P.

Ahern, Jerry
  The quest.—(survivalist: no. 3)
  I. Title
  813'.54[F]   PS3551. H/

  ISBN 0–450–05638–4

To Leslie—a hell of a nifty girl in anybody's book—or with anybody's book.

Chapter 1

Sarah. Michael. Ann. Alive. God—Rourke thought as he walked briskly through the woods beyond the gutted framework of his house, the note Sarah had written and nailed to the barn door folded tightly in his wallet—but why do I need a wallet? Driver's license, Social Security card, concealed weapons permit—the latter made Rourke laugh—he wanted to laugh for the first time since the night of the war. Concealed weapons permit, he laughed again. He walked on, the Python strapped to his right hip in the Ranger leather camouflage rig, the twin stainless Detonics in the Alessi shoulder holsters under his leather jacket, the Colt CAR-15 slung under his right arm, muzzle down, his thumb hooked in the carrying handle under the scope.

It was all useless, he realized, everything in his wallet—or almost everything. The hundred-dollar bill with Ben Franklin looking enigmatic in its center, the CIA card, the credit cards—the only things that were real there anymore was the picture of his wife, Sarah, his son, Michael, and his daughter, Ann—and it wasn't really such a good picture of them, didn't do them justice. But the picture and the voided Rourke family check with the note from Sarah scrawled across it were the only real things ever since the war. Looking up at the stars, he revised his thinking: the stars were real, the earth was still real under his feet, but for how long he didn't know. There had been odd clouds in the night sky, the sunsets had been redder each evening, and the weather seemed definitely to be changing. How many missiles had been launched, bombs dropped that night of World War III, World War Last in all likelihood? And that was another real thing, he thought, puffing on one of the cigars, the stubby, thin tobacco in the left corner of his mouth, almost bolted between his clenched white teeth.

He stopped walking and looked up to the sky again, wondering what was up there. He'd found himself wondering that progressively more often. When he was training to be a physician, he had been concerned with what had made man work, not the humanity but the physiology of it. Later, in the CIA in Covert Operations, he'd been equally concerned with making men stop working: he hadn't become a weapons expert by mere chance or through a correspondence course. Later as a quote/unquote Survival Expert, Rourke had been concerned again with keeping men working—the body functioning and living, despite all odds. But he wondered, as he dragged on the cigar, whether or not Sarah and the children were watching the stars this night, if somewhere there were sanity, somewhere beings who had not pressed the magic and deadly red button and ordered the mass midnight executions of legions of total strangers, men and women and children and all their dogs, cats, frogs, and farm animals. Sometimes, Rourke realized, he almost cursed himself for being sane; it would have been easier the other way.

And there was Paul Rubenstein, the young Jewish guy from New York City, or what had been New York City. He'd never ridden a motor, never fired a gun—let alone in anger—and somehow Rourke counted the younger man his best ally and, next to Sarah and the children, the only friend he had.

He looked at the dark ground, then studied the cigar butt, the tip glowing orange in his fingers, and looked again, trying to find the nearest star.

Rourke didn't like riding the motorcycle in darkness. The Harley Low Rider handled perfectly, everything worked well, but he wouldn't ride any bike without glasses, and all he had were the sunglasses and light sensitive with well-above-normal night vision. Rourke could see well enough in the dark with his sunglasses on, but felt like a fool wearing them. He glanced at his watch. Once he'd crossed into what had been—before the night of the war—the Eastern Time Zone, he'd set the Rolex Submariner one hour ahead. But he still felt he was on Rourke Standard Time: he had set the watch by the sun, but now he was judging sunrise by the watch and the Rolex's luminous face read just past six-thirty A.M. He watched the horizon and could see the reddish line there that meant the clouds were still dust-laden. Radioactive dust? He reminded himself to check one of the two Geiger counters, the one he carried on his bike. He'd left the other one with Paul Rubenstein.

Rourke stopped the bike. He was less than five miles from where he'd left Paul, secure up in the rocks, the wounds still painful but on the mend, the "Schmeisser" subgun as the younger man still insisted on calling the MP-40, the Browning High Power, and Rourke's own Steyr-Mannlicher SSG Special Rifle as companions. Rourke watched the horizon line—the hell with the watch he thought—and saw the sun wink up above the glowing red clouds. The redness of the clouds worried him; he made another mental note to check the radiation count. Suddenly, there was a knot in the pit of his stomach: what would life be like after his quest was through, after he found Sarah, Michael, and Ann? Would they all live in the retreat forever—like early man, but instead in a sophisticated cave with all the conveniences? And afterward, after that, what kind of world—what world at all perhaps—would the children grow up into?

Rourke could see himself, someday saying to his son, "Michael, I leave you vast nuclear wastelands, in which nothing will grow for two centuries, irradiated water you cannot drink, poisoned air you cannot breath, the last surviving Encyclopedia because there is no one left to write another and a superlative command of the language—but no one to talk to. Here's a vintage motorcycle, but there is no gasoline; Here's your choice of the finest pistols ever

10

made, but all the ammunition is gone now. And the birds and the bees I told you about are now totally extinct, and if you do find a human female who hasn't grown up to be a murderess or just gone insane, you can have children with her to perpetuate the race, but it's likely they'll be hideously deformed.'' Rourke shook his head and watched the sunrise. He never knew when it would be the last time anymore. The sun rose because the earth rotated, but when would that stop? He thought of the finishing line for the lecture to his son on the attaining of his manhood: "Have a good time . . .''

Rourke stopped the bike again, the grayness in the East pink-tinged with the color of the horizon, the fog smelling foul and rolling in waves across the ground. He heard shots just ahead, killed the motor on the Harley and swung the CAR-15 from the muzzle down carry across his back into his right hand, the fingers of his fist wrapped around the pistol grip, his left hand automatically coming back and sweeping the bolt open and letting it fly forward, his thumb fingering the semi-automatic's selector into the safe position. The ground dropped off perhaps fifty yards ahead of him. Beyond that was a long grade, then a clearing of flatland, then a high mound of rocks. Rourke edged forward from the Harley, the gunfire growing clearer with each step, sporadic, not like a pitched battle, but rather like . . . He stopped and flattened himself on the lip of the grade. Paul Rubenstein was in the high rocks beyond the clearing where Rourke had left him early that previous night. Below Paul were perhaps a dozen figures, most of them men, but one or two

11

possibly women—(it was hard to tell sometimes, Rourke reflected). The figures—clearly brigands, heavily armed, dirty-looking, and out for blood—were slowly advancing up the rocks, firing to keep Rubenstein pinned down until they could close in. Rourke's face creased into a smile.

"Here it goes again," he whispered.

Chapter 2

Rourke moved the Harley back into a stand of trees, then circled wide around the lip of the grade, noticing five pick up trucks of varying vintage parked perhaps two hundred yards farther back in a small clearing—the brigands' transportation, he decided. Rourke had already assessed the situation. If he started shooting, there would be a protracted gun battle, lasting hours, perhaps it could last days, especially if there were more of the brigands nearby to hear the change in the pattern of the shots and come running to reinforce their friends.

Rourke was now at the far end of the grade, looking down onto the flat expanse leading toward the high rocks. He could see Paul Rubenstein, body tucked down, the Steyr-Mannlicher SSG Special Rifle with the 3 x 9 scope at his shoulder. There would be a series of shots from the brigands to pin Paul down, then the brigands would advance, and

Paul would edge up and fire the green synthetic stocked rifle, then duck down as the brigands shot again. If the brigands had divided themselves into fire-and-maneuver elements, Rourke realized, they could have swept over Paul easily, but fortunately their tactics weren't that good.

Rourke slung the CAR-15 across his back diagonally, muzzle down, and edged over the lip of the grade, hugging the pine trees and low rocks along the side and moving diagonally along the left flank of the attacking brigands. The closest of them—a big man, heavyset, armed with some type of automatic rifle Rourke couldn't immediately identify at the distance—was perhaps fifty yards away, edging along a wall of low rocks running in a zigzag pattern toward the far side of Rubenstein's position. Rourke inched along, flanking the man, but cutting the distance too, timing spurts of his own movements to the covering noise of the brigands' shots. With his left hand, Rourke palmed out the A.G. Russell black chrome Sting IA; the tiny double-edged knife shifted then into his right hand. There was another long round of firing and Rourke made his move, coming up behind the heavy brigand in a rush, diving toward him, tackling the man and bringing him down hard onto the rocks, the squishing sound of the man's head slamming into a rock, Rourke's right fist ramming forward into the throat rather than the man's trunk because of the shortness of the knife blade. Rourke gave the knife a hard twist and ripped it out, flattening himself over the body, listening for a change in the pattern of shooting. Looking up over the low wall of rocks, he saw that nothing had changed. He picked his next target—a tall, lanky man with shoulder-length blond hair and a scraggly beard. Wiping the knife blade clean of blood on the first dead man's trousers, Rourke inched forward over the low rock wall and toward the tall blond man.

The target was twenty-five yards ahead, and as with the first brigand, Rourke waited for another long shot string, then made a headlong dash, leaping over a clump of low rocks, sidestepping a half-rotted pine tree trunk and diving into the man's body just below the waist, throttling him to the ground. Rourke's right hand whipped forward with the knife, his left hand grabbed on to a handful of the greasy hair and jerked the head back to expose the neck, then the knife made a left to right swipe across the unguarded throat. As Rourke drew the knife away, he let the head sag to the rocks. Wiping the blade clean on the blond man's clothes, Rourke spotted his next target, wondering how many of them he could take out before they'd be missed, before someone would turn around, see him, then start the real shooting.

He edged toward a black man, smallish in build, but the bare arms rippling with muscles. A .45 automatic was in the man's left hand. The distance was twenty-five, perhaps thirty yards, the precise range hard to tell because of the man's position in the rocks. Rourke closed to ten yards, waited for another volley of shots from the brigands, then moved forward. He dove toward the man, but the man turned, sidestepping and missing Rourke's knife blade, but Rourke's left arm was solidly hooked on the man's left shoulder and neck and he brought him down. As the man started to shout, Rourke lunged upward from his knees with the Sting IA, the spear point biting deep into the Adam's apple. The man fell back, his mouth half opened, but the scream not coming. The body tumbled backward along the rocks.

Rourke got to his knees, turning, and saw one of the brigands looking his way, starting to shout. Rourke's right hand dropped the knife, flashing toward the Detonics pistol under his left armpit, the tiny stainless steel .45 in his fist, the hammer swiping back to full stand. The first finger of Rourke's right hand edged against the trigger until it gave, the pistol rocking in his hand, the brigand sounding the alarm now falling back, the center of his forehead split wide because of the angle of the 185-grain jacketed hollow point slug when it impacted.

Rourke snatched up his knife, wiped it clean, and holstered it, then pulled the second Detonics from under his right arm.

With one of the .45s in each fist, Rourke started up the sloping rocks, the brigands turning toward him now, directing their fire away from Rubenstein. Rourke fired the gun in the left hand, then the one in the right, then the left again. As the enemy fire started finding him, he dove into the rocks, hearing the chattering of Rubenstein's 9mm subgun coming from the top of the rocks. Jamming both of the emptied .45s into his belt, Rourke swung the CAR-15 from his back, his thumb flicking off the safety, his trigger finger snapping off three-round, semi-automatic bursts from the Colt's thirty-round magazine. The brigands were falling back. Rourke got to his feet and moved out toward them. From the corner of his left eye he saw Rubenstein, moving awkwardly because of the earlier wounds, starting down from the rocks, the subgun in his right hand, the 9mm Browning High Power in his left, both guns spitting fire. Three brigands were still moving along down toward the base of the rocks and past the clearing, heading for the trees. "The pickups," Rourke rasped under his breath. He raised the CAR-15 and fired, then fired again, but the magazine was shot empty and there were still two men running.

Rourke let the CAR-15 swing out of the way under his arm. He snatched the Mag-Na-Ported six-inch Python from his hip, lining the dull metallic finish of the Metalifed gun's front sight into the outlined notch of the Omega rear sight blade, his fists wrapped around the massive Pachmayr grips, the double action pull coming off, a single 158-grain semi-jacketed soft point belching fire at the muzzle. The nearer of the two men was going down and rolling forward, hands outstretched.

Rourke sighted again, fired and missed, then thumb cocked the Python—the last brigand was perhaps seventy-five yards downrange, and Rourke fired, the muzzle climb of the .357 almost negligible, but blocking his view for an instant. As the gun came down out of recoil, he saw the last brigand staggering, both hands clamped to the small of his back, then the legs buckled and the man went down. Rourke turned, swinging the muzzle of the Python around, but eased it down.

Paul Rubenstein was beside him. The younger

17

man, his face streaming sweat, panted, "You shot him in the back." Rourke let the revolver hang limp at his right side along his thigh and said, "Only because that was the guy's best looking side."

Chapter 3

Sarah Rourke dismounted, held loosely one of Tildie's reins as she stood beside the lathered animal, and stared out at the sandbag fence and the farmhouse beyond.

She looked over her shoulder, "Michael, Annie—you, too, Millie—stay here and keep mounted. I'm going to see if there's anyone at that farmhouse." Then looking at ten-year-old Millie Jenkins, she added, "Millie, I want to see if anyone knows your aunt and where I can find her farm."

Sarah turned back and faced the farmhouse, then drying her sweating palms on the sides of her blue-jeaned thighs, she started walking toward the sandbag fence, leading Tildie behind her. The mare whinnied once, snorted, and followed her on the loose rein. Sarah had left tied to Tildie's saddle the modified AR-15 she'd taken from one of the brigands that first morning after the war. All she had was her husband's Colt .45 automatic inside the waistband of her trousers, the butt concealed under her ripped blue T-shirt. She was perspiring despite the fact that it was cool in the Tennessee Mountains. She stripped the blue-and-white bandanna from her hair and shook her dark hair loose as the wind whipped up from beyond the farmhouse.

She had seen no sign of life at the house but it looked normal enough and that was why she had determined to stop. She'd been searching the Smoky Mountains around Mt. Eagle for several days now, trying to find "Aunt Mary" and deliver Millie Jenkins. Aunt Mary was Millie's mother's sister, so the last name would be different and Sarah had no idea what Carla Jenkins's maiden name had been. It was likely, too, Aunt Mary was herself married. All Millie remembered of her aunt's farm was that the house had been set in a valley with a huge horse pasture fenced in behind it and that Aunt Mary grew roses.

As Sarah approached the sandbag fence and stopped, leaning her left hand against one of the sandbags, she stared up at the house, seeing it now in greater detail. There were five pickup trucks parked in the yard, all lined up in some kind of order. The windows of the house were shuttered closed, with narrow slits in them. A chill ran up her spine, but not from the wind, she thought. She reached under her T-shirt and took out her husband's .45. She'd taught herself how to lower the hammer on a loaded chamber and now, with the hammer down, she braced her thumb against it and cocked it, raising the safety, then slid the gun back under her T-shirt, having kept the gun below the level of the sandbags in case anyone in the house was watching her. The slide of the pistol felt almost slimy with her own perspiration.

She climbed up on the bottom stack of sandbags to get a better view of the farmhouse, then raised her right arm, sweeping it back and forth, calling out at the top of her lungs, "Hello! Is anybody there? I want to talk!"

She stopped and listened. There was no reply. She waved the blue-and-white bandanna in her hand and shouted at the top of her voice across the sandbag fence, "Hello! I just want to talk!"

The door of the farmhouse opened. A tall, black-bearded man stepped out onto the unpainted porch, some kind of rifle or shotgun in his hands—Sarah couldn't tell which from the distance. As he walked toward the steps leading up onto the porch, Sarah stopped waving the bandanna.

The man shouted—she could hear him well—"We don't want no strangers 'round heah, lady. Git out a' heah!"

Sarah Rourke shook her head angrily, too angry to say anything. Then, forcing herself under control, she said, "Look, I've got three small children with me. I don't want anything from you—just directions. Please!"

"Git out! Them's directions, lady." And the man started to turn and walk away.

All the tension, all the fear, all the loneliness and frustration welled up inside her, and she fought to hold back tears. She screamed at the man, "Please! For God's sake!"

The man walked another step or two, then turned, waited, then walked back toward the end of the porch.

"There's a gate down yonder. Send yer young'ns along ahead of y'all—and no tricks."

She sank against the sandbags, waving her right hand and shouting, "Thank you!"

She looked back at the children and suddenly felt very tired.

"Thank you," she muttered again, but not to the man on the porch.

Chapter 4

"There're brigands all over here," Rourke said, his voice low. His eyes squinted behind the sunglasses against the bright morning sunlight.

"Do you think they found your retreat, John?" young Paul Rubenstein asked, pushing his wire-framed glasses back from his nose, his face perspiring profusely.

Rourke thought a moment, then said, "No, that's the least of my worries. Maybe an archeologist will find it a thousand years from now, but nobody's going to find it today, tomorrow, or twenty years from now. Trouble is—" Rourke looked past Rubenstein and beyond the rocks where the bodies of the brigands they had killed lay—"I wonder if twenty years from now I'm still going to be living in it."

"What do you mean, John?"

Rourke lit one of his small cigars, thinking

momentarily about the cigars he had stored at the retreat. "What I mean, Paul, is the world—you look at the sunsets, the sunrises, the way the weather has been hot one day, cold the next, the rains, the winds? And if the world stays in one piece, what happens then? Can we rebuild? There are so many questions. Not enough of them have answers and the ones that do are tough answers."

Rourke stopped talking and looked down at the Colt Python. He'd reloaded the other guns and now slipped the spent cartridges, identifying them from the primer indentations from the cylinder and replacing them with some of the loose rounds he carried. He stood up from the crouch and stretched, snatching up the CAR-15 and slinging it under his right shoulder.

"But," Rourke continued with a sigh, "as somebody once said out of frustration and bitter experience, life goes on, hmm?" Rourke, without waiting for Paul, started walking across the flat expanse at the top of the rock cluster toward where he and the still recuperating Rubenstein had hauled the younger man's bike that previous night. Rourke scanned the ground below. In the darkness they had manhandled the bike up into the rocks, but now, with the light, Rourke saw a path—precarious, but he judged it manageable. "You wait here," he said, looking back over his shoulder toward Rubenstein.

Rourke picked his way across the rocks and stopped beside the bike, then looked back toward the path, and reassessed his judgment that the bike could be driven down. He glanced at the Rolex on his left wrist, then at the sun. With the gunfire ceased and the brigands not having returned to the larger force Rourke felt they were a part of, he decided it was only a matter of time before someone came—perhaps a heavily armed brigand force.

Rourke did not want that. He was too close to the retreat to waste the time, he thought, and eager to begin searching for Sarah and the children. He smiled, "eager." From the night he had stood talking with the RCMP Inspector in Canada and the man's wife had turned on the radio newsbroadcast, Rourke had been more than eager. When he took the first flight out to Atlanta, the bombing and missile strikes had begun. In the long night after the plane was diverted and before the crash of the jetliner in New Mexico—and in the long days and nights since—Rourke had thought of little else than finding his family.

He had resolved early on to be unwavering on one point—that somehow they had survived. And they had. As he mounted the bike and started the engine, the corners of his mouth turned down in a bitter smile. He looked out across the land from the high ground. If Sarah and the children were somewhere in the mountains of northern Georgia, they would be hard to find. Were they somewhere else in Georgia, the Carolinas, perhaps Tennessee? Every mile they traveled likely took them farther away, he realized, making the search just that much longer and more difficult.

Finding a woman and two young children, refugees in a country full of refugees—The entire midsection of the country was a radioactive desert. There was no law. What of the Russians, the brigands—God knew what that lay out there? Rourke revved the bike, squinted against the sun and, using his combat booted feet to support the machine rumbling between his legs, started it down the path.

Chapter 5

It was never good to let them see you looking dejected, KGB Maj. Vladmir Karamatsov reminded himself, throwing his shoulders back as he stepped to the door of the military aircraft and breathed the cool night air of Chicago. At the base of the short ladder leading down from the jet was his staff car, his chauffeur who was waiting on the runway tarmac beside it, snapped to attention as he saw his superior.

Karamatsov smiled as he nimbly jumped the last few steps of the ladder, then tossed his leather dispatch case in a gentle arc to his subordinate.

The driver caught the case, saluted, and said, "Good evening, Comrade Major."

"Good evening, Piotr," Karamatsov responded without looking at the man. He stared at the runway lights at the far end of the field instead. More military transports were arriving. He reflected that

27

they would be needed. After the loss of the new American President, Samuel Chambers, and the dangerous and embarrassing episode with John Rourke and his own wife, Natalia, Karamatsov had revised his earlier impressions of American pacification following the war that his country had nominally won. A nation of armed citizens, a nation of individualists—it would be hard to quell their resistance. He had learned that.

Rather than bombing the cities, Karamatsov thought, smiling almost bitterly, they should have bombed the countryside. Bombing the countryside would have been easier in the final analysis, since the people of the cities would have been easier to subjugate. He had seen no point in bombing New York out of existence, for example. The wealth of the city was eternally lost now, and the weaponless, fear-ridden people of the American giant would have been easier to subjugate than the heavily armed and fiercely independent Westerners and Southerners.

He noticed himself shrugging his shoulders as Piotr, his driver, said, "Comrade Major, there is something?"

"No, Piotr," Karamatsov said and turned, his dark eyes gleaming. "I was just considering the efficiency with which our leaders are introducing additional troops to aid in the pacification of the United States. We are fortunate indeed to be possessed of such men of courage and foresight. Is this not so, Piotr?"

"Yes, Comrade Major," the young man said. A smile forced on his face, Karamatsov thought.

The KGB major and the Army corporal eyed each

other a moment, Karamatsov still thinking in English, saying in his mind, "The boy doesn't believe that bullshit any more than I do." He laughed, then walked toward his open car door, and stepped inside the Cadillac. He liked American cars: they ran, which was more, he thought, than could be said of their Soviet counterparts.

Undoing the holsterless belt on his greatcoat, then undoing the double row of buttons, he slumped back in the seat, taking the proffered dispatch case from Piotr. "To the house, Piotr." He removed his hat, setting it on the seat beside him on top of the dispatch case, and closed his eyes, waiting for the motion of the car to start as soon as his luggage was removed from the plane and placed in the trunk of the car.

He opened his eyes and sat up, startled. The car was slowing down, and he sat forward in the rear seat to look over the front seat through the tinted glass of the windshield. He could see the house. Large, white-painted brick with a low porch and three steps leading from it toward a walk that jutted out to a cemented driveway slicing between dead grass patches that once had been verdant lawns, he imagined.

The square footage of the house was over three thousand, larger by far than anything he and Natalia had ever lived in. At one time, the suburb of Chicago, where the house was situated, had been for the very rich. Now they were dead or had fled. All houses within the six-block area had been taken over as an officer's compound or for important civilian officials, falling into both categories, really.

Karamatsov thought he had gotten one of the best of the houses.

As the Cadillac Fleetwood turned up the driveway, Karamatsov leaned back, minutely inspecting the insignia on his hat, but really wondering what it would be like with Natalia. It would be the first private time they had had since the events leading to Chambers's and Rourke's escape from the complex in the taken-over air base in Texas. He had covered for her, partially he realized because she knew enough about him to damn him and partially—

The car stopped and Karamatsov put on his hat, waiting for his chauffeur to open his door. Had Rourke lied, he asked himself? Had Rourke and Natalia been lovers?

"What sir?" Piotr asked.

Karamatsov half turned to face the younger man as he stood beside the door. Karamatsov stopped, frozen almost half-bent as he stepped from the back seat of the car. "Nothing, Piotr, nothing." Karamatsov stepped out of the car, his great coat unbuttoned, his belt over his arm beside the dispatch case. "I will need you at six A.M. Have a pleasant evening."

"You too, Comrade Major, a pleasant evening."

Looking up at the lighted windows in the house, thinking about the woman inside, anger suddenly boiled within him. Karamatsov muttered, "Yes. Thank you, Piotr." Turning on his heel, he added, "The bags—place them just inside the doorway and you may leave."

"Yes, Comrade Major."

Karamatsov stood at the base of the steps, watching Piotr pass him to go up to the door, ring the bell and wait—a flight bag, a large briefcase and a suit bag in his arms.

The door opened. Karamatsov could not see her, only hear the voices.

Piotr said, "Good evening, Comrade."

"Good evening, Piotr, " the soft contralto responded.

Karamatsov balled his right fist. He imagined her with closed eyes. She liked white, and she was probably wearing a white robe over a white negligee. She would be impeccably beautiful as she was always—the bright dark-blue eyes, the almost black hair, the ivory white of the skin that lost any suntan almost immediately to return to the almost religious alabaster radiance. She would be smiling at Piotr; she always smiled at people. That was part of why she was the best agent he knew in KGB: she was coldly efficient and deadly, but there was a warmth and humanness in her when business was not the order of the day. Even her enemies had always found it hard to hate her.

He walked up the steps and stopped at the small porch, looking over Piotr as he set down the baggage and staring at Natalia, his wife.

"Good evening, Natalia," he murmured.

"Good evening, Vladmir," she answered, her eyes downcast.

She was wearing white, something with lace that she had not acquired in the Soviet Union, something beautiful. She looked the model wife—elegant, lovely, almost shy and demure. She remained unmoving as Piotr came to attention between them.

"Good night, Piotr," Karamatsov said.

Piotr looked awkward. It had suddenly become common knowledge that Karamatsov and Natalia were married, a fact Karamatsov had concealed for years, and the looks of awkwardness in the eyes of those who knew them, however casually, were something he was becoming accustomed to.

Natalia said nothing. Piotr moved between them and stepped out, saluting as Karamatsov waved him away. The door closed behind Karamatsov's hand as he leaned against it. Natalia was still staring at the floor; he could not see her eyes.

"You are radiant tonight. You are radiant every night, but you know that," he whispered hoarsely. Stepping away from the door, he stripped the black leather gloves from his hands and set them along with his hat and dispatch case on the small leather-covered table by the door. He slipped off the great-coat and draped it across a French provincial chair beside the table.

"A drink, please?" he asked.

She said nothing, but moved away. Because of the flowing quality of the lace-trimmed floor length robe she wore, it seemed she floated to the kitchen rather than walked, he thought.

He unbuttoned his uniform tunic and removed it, dropping it on the side of a sofa as he stepped down three steps into the living room. He undid the top buttons of his white shirt, automatically checking the tiny S & W Model 36 holstered inside his trouser band on his left hip.

He turned, seeing Natalia re-enter from the kitchen with a tray containing a bottle of vodka and a glass.

"The ever dutiful wife," he remarked as she passed him and bent over a low coffee table to set down the bottle and glass. "You aren't drinking?"

"I don't feel like it, Vladmir," she said quietly.

His hands held her shoulders and he snapped her around to him. Her dark hair fell across her forehead as her head bent back, tossing the hair from her face showing her slender white neck. His right hand moved to her throat and tightened around it.

"You're hurting me."

Karamatsov laughed. "You are a martial arts expert; why don't you stop me?" he asked, then let go of her neck, bent down and poured a glass of vodka for himself and downed half the tumbler. He looked at her. "I want you to have a drink." He knotted the fingers of his right hand in the hair at the nape of her neck and bent her head back, arching her back. Her mouth contorted downward. Karamatsov raised the glass to her mouth, forced its rim between her lips, and poured the vodka from the glass, some of the liquid dribbling down the sides of her mouth. He let go of her hair as she started to cough, choking on the vodka.

Her head bent low over her knees, one hand held her hair from her face as she sat perched on the edge of the sofa.

He bent down, staring at her. "Did you drink with Rourke, Natalia? Do you like American whiskey better than Russian vodka?"

He half stood, poured another glass of the vodka for himself, studied the clear liquid for an instant. He suddenly raked the back of his right hand

33

downward, his knuckles connecting against the miraculously perfect right cheek of the seated woman in front of him. The force of his hand knocked her from the edge of the couch onto the floor.

"I did not cheat on you with Rourke. He wouldn't," she said, staring up at Karamatsov from the floor.

Karamatsov dropped to his knees, spilling half the vodka from his glass, wetting the front of his shirt and pants. His face inches from hers, he rasped, "But you wanted to!"

His right fist lashed out, and her left cheekbone suddenly lost its perfection as well.

Chapter 6

Varakov stared at the skeletons of the mastodons in the main hall. In the weeks since Soviet Military Headquarters for North America had been set up in the former lake-front museum, General Varakov had grown exceedingly fond of watching the two extinct giants. And sometimes when he looked at them, he thought, an amused smile crossing his florid thick lips, instead of mastodons he saw the skeletons of a bear and an eagle locked in mortal combat eons after their disappearance from the earth. He looked up through the windows over the far door. There was darkness.

Gen. Ishmael Varakov had always liked the dark; it was peaceful, yet full of things to come.

"Comrade General?"

Varakov turned from the railing overlooking the main gallery and smiled at his young woman secretary. "They are here?"

35

"Yes, Comrade General."

He shrugged, looked at his unbuttoned uniform tunic, then left it unbuttoned, reminding himself he was the commanding general and there was no one for thousands of miles who had the power to tell him to button it. "Go tell them I'll be there." He turned to look back at the mastodons once more. If nothing else positive had come out of the war, he thought, it was seeing this place. When he had served as an advisor once in Egypt, he had never seen such treasures of the past as were there. He had never appreciated the beauty and complexity—yet at once simplicity— of the evolution of nature as he had from what he had seen here. He wandered the halls incessantly. He had at last found a home he liked, he thought, smiling. Then out loud he added, "Here among the rest of the anomalies of antiquity." He smacked his lips, turned from the railing, and started toward the low, winding steps leading to the main floor and the meeting.

He shuffled on his sore feet past a bronze of a stone age man, another of a Malaysian woman, and another of a bushman armed with a blowgun. He turned right toward his wall-less office just off the main hall. An office without walls was the best kind, he thought with a smile. They were all there, the ranking general and field-grade officers of his command, sitting in a neat semicircle facing his empty desk. He stopped and watched them, shook his head, and stared at his feet, then smiling, walked ahead, rumbling, "There is no need to disturb yourselves, gentlemen. Please remain seated."

He crossed past the semicircle of men on the edges

of their seats, rounded the corner of his desk and plopped into his chair. He leaned forward across the leather desk top, then pushed off his shoes, his white stockinged toes splaying against the carpet under them.

"We all are aware," he began, looking at no one in particular, "that the complete military occupation of the United States is impossible at this point in time. Those fragmented units of American, British, and West German troops and others are still making life in Europe miserable for our forces. China is holding its borders and we are holding ours—a land war with China, gentlemen, would be madness. I am convinced we would never have occupied this land if it weren't for the fact that we need the industrial output possible from the still-standing factories— weapons, small arms, tanks, food, chemicals. And this—" and he hammered his fist on the desk top— "is our primary mission in the United States. I emphasize this because many reports have come to me that it seems instead we are bent on the total pacification of America. That is not within the realm of possibility at this point in time—regardless of official line, it is not!"

He leaned back and stared past the men. "I have decided to take personal charge of the fine details of the plan for civilian pacification. It is a limited plan to achieve limited and realistic goals, Comrades. Since the restarting of vital industries and their protection from sabotage is our most important goal, we shall act accordingly. I shall borrow something from the psychology and experience of the very people we are attempting to control—and I emphasize control.

Control! I have signed an order establishing what can best be called forts, military outposts designed to be as largely self-sufficient as possible, like the American frontier outposts we have all seen in the American Indian capitalist exploitation films. We—" he leaned forward, raising his first finger on each hand, staring briefly into the eyes of each of the men in the semi circle before him—"we will be the cavalry! Our functions will be simple—to prevent the rise of organized resistance and protect the civilian population as well. Notice that: protect the civilian population. There are bands of blood thirsty brigands prowling this land, killing and looting. We must prove to the surviving American civilian population that we are not out to facilitate their extermination; we must protect them from these brigands, and at the same time we must realize that some of these brigand forces could become the kernel around which massive armed resistance can grow. As a formal resistance movement develops—and much of my intelligence information indicates this may already be happening—we must be so actively engaged in protecting the American people from these criminal brigand elements that we can lump together these resistance fighters with the lawless brigand elements and combat them all. We must not let resistance become a popular movement as it did in Afghanistan, or years earlier as it did for the Nazis—" he almost spat out the word— "as they fought the French."

For the first time one of his subordinate officers, General Novadkhastovski, spoke.

"Comrade General," he began, then his face

softened into a smile as he glanced around the room. "Ishmael. We are to protect these people?"

"That is right, Illya, we will never, not within our lifetimes at least—" he stared past his old wartime friend to the bony mastodons in the main hall near the fountain beyond—" but if we can make them see that their safety," he stopped, realizing he had skipped an entire portion of his idea (he was getting old, he sighed) then backtracked—"we will never get them to like us, to willingly accept our rule, but if we can at least make them rely on us for their safety we will have won the most major of psychological battles. And, as long as the brigands are roaming free, we too must worry about their harassment. These gangs of ruffians are heavily armed and kill without mercy. They are animals."

"It is wise, I think. You are right, Ishmael."

Varakov nodded to his old friend. Such a thing for the man to say was worth more than an official commendation; he valued the man's mind.

"Thank you, old friend," Varakov said. "The first of these forts will be established in northeastern Georgia." There were smiles because of the similarities in Soviet Georgia and American Georgia—but in the name only. "It will be charged with patrolling northeastern Georgia and the Carolinas and extending to the Atlantic Coast." And then Varakov laughed. "We have given Florida with its sinkholes, forest fires, diminished water table and rising coastline, etc., to the Cubanos. And as our loyal allies we wish them well!"

There was a broad round of laughter, even Varakov's usually reserved secretary smiling, almost blushing as she sat on the small chair by the side of his desk taking notes on the meeting. As the laughter subsided, Varakov cleared his throat, then began again. "This fort will be located in what I understand is one of the oldest universities in the United States. I would encourage that this structure remain as unaltered as possible. If we appear to show respect for what the American people themselves respect, perhaps we too can gain some of this respect, if not affection." Then Varakov looked at his secretary, saying, "Call in Colonel Korcinski. We need him now."

The young woman got up, smoothing down what Varakov thought was an overly long uniform skirt, then walked across the open-walled office and out to the main hall. She returned in a moment, following discreetly behind Col. Vassily Korcinski. The Colonel was middle-aged, white-haired, handsome to the point of effeminacy, Varakov thought. He leafed through Korcinski's service record file—airborne qualified, wounded twice in combat, married with two teenage sons in Moscow. They were still alive and had survived the American attack, the file noted. Varakov wanted no man in a position of authority with a personal vendetta.

Korcinski stood at attention before the desk, and Varakov nodded to him, saying to the assembled staff officers, "Gentlemen, the Commander of our first outpost!"

Chapter 7

Natalia reeled under her husband's blow to her left cheek. His knuckles were bloodied. She stared up at him. She started to her feet, saw his hand coming for her again, and tried to raise her hand against the blow, but he knocked her right arm away with his left hand and his right fist crashed down against the side of her face. She sprawled back across the couch, somehow feeling indecent that her robe and nightgown had bunched up past her hips. She looked at Vladmir's eyes, watched him watching her, felt the tears welling up in her eyes, then shrank back as she saw him undo his uniform belt and draw the heavy leather from the trouser loops. He picked up the vodka bottle.

"I have decided, Natalia," he said, his voice low, edged with tension and trembling. "I will have you and that way I will know if someone else has had you." He tilted the square bottle upward and she watched the colorless liquid pour from the narrow glass neck into his mouth and his Adam's apple move as he swallowed. She edged back along the couch, pulling down at the hem of her gown.

Karamatsov laughed, throwing the half-empty bottle across the room, then reached toward her. She tried to push away, edging back. Then his right hand clenching the belt, swung back past his left shoulder and slashed downward, and she screamed as the leather stung against her legs. She cringed, burrowing into the couch, feeling the sting of the leather on her bare behind, then feeling her husband's hands pulling her up. She was on her feet but looked away from his eyes. He had been like a father, yet a lover, her leader as she grew into her womanhood, the only man to have her. Now she could not look into his eyes. She felt the belt swish lazily against her flesh and his hands at the neckline of her gown, the robe open now. There was a tearing sound, and her neck and shoulders ached. She realized her eyes were closed. She opened them as he stripped away the tatters of her nightclothes. Automatically, her right arm crossed the nipples of her breasts and her left hand cupped over the triangle of hair at her crotch.

"Vladmir, please," she begged.

"No," he answered so softly she could barely hear him.

She watched the belt starting up again and tried to move aside, but his left fist crashed into her stomach and she doubled over, dropping to her knees on the carpet. Then she felt the belt across her back, felt his hand in her hair as though it were being ripped out by the roots, her head drawn back and her neck bent back to where she could barely breathe.

She looked finally into Vladmir's eyes. He said, "You won't fight." The belt, looped double in his right hand, lashed across her left cheek and the bridge of her nose and, as her left hand went to her face, it came away bloodied. She couldn't open her left eye.

His left hand was still knotted in her hair and he hauled her to her feet, then shoved her back onto the couch. He stood over her, his hands dropping the belt to open his uniform trousers, pushing them down as he fell on top of her.

"No," she whimpered. Then she turned her eyes away. She felt his hands on her, pulling at her breasts, his fingers knotting in the hair at her crotch, then his hands coming inside her.

"No," she murmured, then felt the hardness stabbing into her. "No!" she screamed. She stared up at the ceiling until he finally sank against her. Tears streamed down her face, but she felt she wasn't crying.

After a long while, she heard him mutter, "Bitch—unfeeling bitch." His right hand cuffed her face, then his left, then his right. Her mouth was bleeding, and she tried to raise her head because she was choking on the blood.

He was standing, reeling, the vodka bottle was back in his hand, some of the clear liquid somehow still inside, then he tilted the bottle. A smile—something like she had never seen—crossed his lips as he picked up the belt, looked at the bottle in his other hand, then lashed out with the belt, the heavy leather almost instantly raising a dark red welt across her breasts. He knocked her back to the couch, the bottle still in his hand.

The neck of the bottle was pointed toward her, held low, and she stared at it with her good right eye through the tears.

Vladmir Karamatsov whispered, "If I do not please you, then perhaps this will." And he laughed as he started toward her.

Natalia screamed, gagging on the salty taste of the blood in her mouth, her puffed and cracked lips drawn back in horror.

Chapter 8

"I don't know," Rourke said, not looking at Rubenstein, but staring up at the stars. They were less than a mile from the principal entrance to the retreat. "Sometimes you get the feeling there's something happening, you don't know where or what, but that you're involved with it anyway, and that someday you'll learn what it was and when—sort of like the feeling you get when a shiver runs up your spine and people say that somebody's just walked across your grave. Maybe they have."

"What do you mean?" Paul Rubenstein asked, his voice sounding tired.

"I don't know," Rourke almost laughed. "Come on. Not much farther now." Rourke looked at the balding younger man in the starlight. Rubenstein was exhausted, his wounds still depleting his strength. The road to the entrance of the retreat was twisted and difficult. "Come on."

They rode the bikes, the engines barely above stalling, up the narrow pathway. Rourke eyed the familiar landmarks; he knew each tree and each rock. He had found the site of the retreat six years before, purchased it, then over the last three years was able to afford to convert it. It was a natural cave, carved over millions of years by the forty-foot-high waterfall from an underground spring, filtering from the natural pool at its base down into the rocks, coursing below in a narrowing cavern to God-knew-where—its origins, he guessed, perhaps as far away as the Canadian border, the water icy cold, crystal clear, perhaps only coming to light as it passed through the rear of the cave. He could mark the places where the waterfall had been over the millions of years since it had begun, how it had gradually carved out the cave. Giant stalactites were suspended from the cave ceiling and gradually bled their substance to form the stalagmites below them.

He used the underground portion of the stream as his hydro-electric power source, his own generators capable of supplying three times his maximum power needs. He had left the structure of the cave basically unaltered, the natural rise at the rear of the cave to the waterfall's right forming the main sleeping quarters, smaller natural mezzanines forming the additional rooms: two more bedrooms, the kitchen, and the bath, the latter shielded from the rest of the massive cave by a natural, opaque curtain of limestone. Rourke had electrified the cavern, plumbed it and, using a four-wheel drive pickup truck, gradually furnished it with appliances, bedroom furnishings, everything that would be needed to preserve the comfort if he were ever forced to live permanently in the retreat. Spare parts, service manuals, all were carefully catalogued and stored. The great room was the room he liked. It was the main body of the cavern and its rear was formed by the pool at the base of the waterfall. In this room were his books, records, videotape library, guns—his room, he had always thought of it. As he slowed his borrowed Harley Low Rider and signaled Paul Rubenstein to do the same, he almost felt a longing for the place, a sense of normalcy there.

"We're here," Rourke whispered.

"Where? I don't see anything."

"You're not supposed to." Then Rourke explained. "Once I had the retreat I realized it would be useless to me if I couldn't absolutely rely on the fact that it wouldn't be discovered. That meant I had to have some sort of secret entrance. In comic books, movies, science fiction, they put branches or shrubs in front of the cave entrance, but none of that works. I wanted something more permanent."

"So what did you do?" Rubenstein asked.

"Watch." Rourke dismounted from the bike and walked toward the cracked and rough weathered granite wall before them. He looked down; they were approximately half way up the mountainside. He walked to a large boulder on the right of his bike, then pushed against it with his hands. The boulder rolled away. He walked to his far left where a similar, but squared-off rock butted against the granite face. "See," Rourke began, pushing on it. "This whole area of Georgia is built on a huge granite plate at varying depths. This mountain is an outcropping of it, extending all the way into Tennessee, maybe well beyond. I did a lot of research in archeology to come up with this—how the Egyptian tombs were sealed off, Mayan temples." Rourke braced himself against the rock and pushed it aside.

There was rumbling in the rock itself, and Rubenstein drew back. The rock on which Rourke stood began to sink, and as it did a slab of rock about the size of a single-car-garage door began to slide inward. "Just weights and counterbalances," Rourke said, smiling, his face reflected by the starlight. "When you want to open from inside, levers perform the same function as moving the rocks out here."

Rubenstein leaned forward, peering into the gradually opening doorway and the darkness beyond.

"Come on," Rourke said, then walked into the darkness. Rubenstein was off his bike now, but Rourke saw the young man standing unnecessarily close behind him. "It's fine—really."

A flashlight was in Rourke's left hand, one of the angleheads the two men had stolen from the geological supply house in Albuquerque. As the weak beam shone against the granite, Rourke bent down, then flicked a switch with an audible click. A dim light, reddish in hue, illuminated the cavern opening.

"Get your bike inside."

Rourke went back outside to get his Harley and wheeled it through the entrance. As Rubenstein began to move his machine, Rourke rasped, "Paul, there's a redhandled lever in there, by the light switch. Swing it down and lock it under the notch."

Rourke waited a moment, looking up at the stars, then heard Rubenstein shout, "Got it, John."

Rourke said nothing, but bent and rolled the two rock counterbalances into position, then stepped into the cave. He bent to the redhandled lever, loosed it safely from the notch retaining it and raised it, the granite doorway started to move, the rock beneath them shuddering audibly.

"Relax," Rourke said softly, turned, and saw Rubenstein staring beyond at the edge of the red light to the steel double doors at the far end of the antechamber. "I've got ultrasonics installed to prevent insects or vermin from getting in—closed circuit TV up there," Rourke said, gesturing above their heads to the low stone ceiling.

Rourke walked to the steel doors, shone his flashlight on the combination dials and began to manipulate them, then turned the lever-shaped handles and the doors swung open.

"Paul," Rourke said, stepping into the darkness, "kill that light switch for red back there, huh?"

Rourke stepped into the darkness, reached out his right hand and waited until he assumed Rubenstein was beside him in the darkness. He could see the light of the anglehead flashlight.

"Now," Rourke almost whispered, then got the light switch.

"God!"

Rourke looked at the younger man, smiled, and stepped down into the great room. "Just as I described it," Rourke said with what he felt was justifiable pride. "Let's bring the bikes down the ramp." Rourke pointed to his left to the far side of the three broad stone steps leading into the great room, "then I'll give you a fast tour before you collapse."

Rubenstein wiped his brow. Rourke started to back up the three steps, then into the darkness beyond the steel doors. Rourke started his liberated Harley down the ramp, stopped it, went back and closed the doors from the inside, sliding a bar in place on levers across the double doors.

"Place is stone, so it's fireproof, everything in it is as fireproof as possible. I've got a couple of emergency exits too; show 'em to you tomorrow." Rourke returned to the Harley and started it down the ramp, stopping again to hit another light switch mounted against the cave wall, metal wire molding running from it up toward the darkness of the ceiling. The ramp was wide enough for the two men to walk their bikes side by side. In front of them, at the base of the ramp, Rourke pointed out a truck.

"Ford—four-wheel-drive pickup, converted it to run off pure ethyl alcohol. Got a distillery for it set up on the far side over there." Rourke pointed well beyond the camouflage-painted pickup truck to the far end of the side cavern. Along the natural rock wall separating it from the main cavern were rows upon rows of shelves, stacked floor to ceiling, several large ladders spaced along their length.

"Up there, spare ammunition—reloading components when I get to that—food, whiskey, whatever."

Rourke parked the bike on its stand. Rubenstein did the same. Rourke walked the length of the side cavern, pointing to the shelves.

"I've got a complete inventory that I run on an ascending/descending balance system so I know what's running down, what might spoil, etc." Then Rourke started pinpointing, calling off the things on the shelves. "Toilet paper, paper towels, bath soap, shampoo and conditioner, candles, light bulbs—sixties, hundreds—fluorescent tubes—lightswitches, screws, nails, bolts, nuts, washers—" he stopped to point to a low shelf—"McCulloch Pro Mac 610 chain saw—best there is, combines easy handling with near professional quality durability—spare parts, etc." Rourke moved on. "All the ammunition for my guns." Rourke started at .22 Long Rifle, moved up to .38 Special, then .357 Magnum, 9mm Parabellum, .44 Magnum, and .45 ACP, then the rifle cartridges—.223 and .308—then twelve-gauge shotgun shells, double 0 buck and rifled slugs, mostly two and three-quarter-inch. "I stick to the shorter stuff," Rourke commented, "because it works in the three-inch Magnums, not vice-versa."

There was row upon row of Mountain House foods in large containers and small packages, some ordinary canned goods, other food supplies, then stacks of white bootsocks, underpants, handkerchiefs. "All reserve stuff," Rourke commented. A large bin occupied some of the end of the shelving area, inside it, as Rourke showed Rubenstein, were holsters, slings, various other leather goods. Beyond this was a shelf filled with a dozen pair of black GI combat boots, and beside these a half dozen pairs of rubber thongs.

"It'll take you a while," Rourke commented to

51

Rubenstein, "before you can really see all I've put up, but you'll catch on to it. Check the inventory sheets." Rourke took down one of four clipboards hanging on hooks at the far end of the shelving. "Now look behind you. My pride and joy—" Rourke gestured to the far wall, a gleaming black Harley-Davidson Low Rider suspended a few inches off the floor—"to protect the tires."

Rourke walked back to the end of the shelf row and hit another switch and the side cavern behind them went dark. Rourke hit a second switch and the darkened smaller chamber ahead of them illuminated.

Rourke commented, "Work room," and pointed along the walls and down a row of log tables. Vises, reloading equipment, power saws, drill press, then ranked on shelves above these were oil filters, spark plugs, fan belts, tools hung on pegboard wall panels beyond these. Rourke set his CAR-15 on one of the tables, withdrew the six-inch Python, setting it beside the rifle, next he snatched both Detonics stainless pistols from their double-shoulder rig and set them down as well, then the small A.G. Russell black chrome Sting IA.

"Gotta clean these tomorrow," Rourke observed.

Rubenstein took the Browning High Power from his belt and set it down, then laid down the Schmeisser, "I'll get the little Lawman and the Steyr later," Rourke noted. "Come on."

Rourke walked past the rows of tables and hit the light switch, then turned a corner and, once again, they were in the main cavern, but at the far end of the great room, the sound of the waterfall splashing beside them.

Rourke stripped away his leather jacket, his Alessi shoulder rig, and the Ranger leather belt, and set them on the arm of what looked like a leather-covered chair.

"Vinyl," Rourke observed. "Hate the stuff, but it's less susceptible to damage than leather and more easily repaired."

Rourke started into the room, then stopped, turned to Rubenstein, and took off his sunglasses. "What would you like to see first? I bet, the bathroom, hmm? How about a real shower?"

Rourke didn't wait for an answer, but started toward the near side of the great room, walked up a row of three low stone steps and pointed toward the opaque curtain of stone. "In there—help yourself. Grab yourself some clothes. I'll use it later."

Then Rourke turned and walked across the great room toward the television set, the stereo, the books, the guns. He stopped in front of the glass gun case and slid the glass panel aside. He heard Rubenstein's voice behind him, turned, and saw him with a handful of clean clothes. Rourke smiled, pleased the younger man had found his way back to his motorcycle, already learning to make his way around the retreat.

"What's that, John?"

"Come and see," Rourke said, staring back at the cabinet. He heard Rubenstein stop beside him, then pointed at each weapon in the gun case. "That's an Interdynamics KG-9 9mm assault pistol," Rourke began.

"Looks like a submachine gun," Rubenstein commented.

"Only a semi-automatic, though," Rourke said, then pointed to each succeeding item, identifying it in turn, "Smith and Wesson Model 29 six-inch, Metalifed and Mag-Na-Ported; Smith and Wesson Model 60 two-inch stainless Chiefs .38 Special; Colt Mk IV, Series '70 Government Model; Metalifed with a Detonics Competition Recoil system installed and Pachmayr Colt Medallion grips. That little thing is an FIE .38 Special chrome Derringer, and the little tubes on the shelf down here are .22 Long Rifle and .25 ACP barrel inserts made by Harry Owens of Sport Specialties. Makes the little gun able to fire .38 Special, .22 rimfire, or .25 ACP. I've got more of those insert barrels for my Detonics, for my shotguns, et cetera." Rourke pointed back up to the cabinet. "That gun is a Colt Official Police .38 Special five-inch—Metalifed with Pachmayr grips. Same frame essentially as a Python, so I had it reamed out to .357 to increase its versatility." Then Rourke moved to his right to the long guns, racked one over the other. "That's a standard AR-15, no scope. That's a Mossberg 500ATP6P Parkerized riot shotgun. Safariland sling on it. That's an original Armalite AR-7 .22 Long Rifle. Take it apart and it stows in the buttstock, even floats. Had enough?"

Rourke turned, smiling at Rubenstein.

"How much—I mean it's rude, John, I know that but how—"

"Every cent I could scrape together for the last six years, after the cost of the property itself. I gambled. I'm sorry I won, but it paid off I guess." Rourke closed the case and walked toward the sofa in the center of the great room, then leaned down to a small box on the table, and looked inside. "Empty," he muttered, and crossed the room.

He glanced over his shoulder, Rubenstein following him. Rourke smiled, saying, "You're more curious than eager for that shower, aren't you?"

Rourke kept walking, up the three low stone steps and into the kitchen. There was a long counter with stools beside it, on the other side a six-burner range with a double oven, a double-door refrigerator, and more counter space. At the far left were two chest-type white freezers. "I've got a big meat locker back in the side of the utility area, maybe you saw it—this is for stuff that is most commonly used."

Rubenstein was next to him as Rourke opened one of the freezers, the entire left half of it was filled with aluminum-foil-wrapped packages. Rourke took a package from the freezer and turned over a roast, looked at it, then closed the freezer. He unwrapped the package on top of the freezer, extracted one of the small cigars he liked, rolled it between his fingers, smelled it, and put it to his mouth. He lit it with the Zippo.

"You're kidding," Rubenstein said, his voice sounding to Rourke as though the young man were shocked.

"What's the matter? What's so strange? All the comforts of home." Rourke stopped, the lighter still burning in his hand as he stared over Rubenstein's shoulder, past the counter to the small table on the side of the couch. There was a picture there—he couldn't see it, but knew it—of Sarah and the children. "Almost all the comforts," he said, his voice low. He snapped closed the cowling of the lighter and dropped the lighter in his pocket.

"How did you get this up here?"

"With the truck," Rourke answered, as he went to the refrigerator, opened it, and took out an ice tray. He took a large glass beer mug from an overhead cabinet and filled it half with ice. He replaced the unused ice cubes, muttering, "Help yourself to anything you want," then turned on a small black switch next to the sink. There was a rumble, a mechanical hum, then Rourke turned on the cold water faucet, the spigot sputtering a moment. "Air gets in the system," Rourke remarked, then water spattered out, and Rourke walked away, leaving the water running.

He went to another cabinet, this time below the counter level, and extracted a half-gallon bottle of Seagram's 7, twisted off the cap, breaking the stamp, and poured a good three inches in the beer mug over the ice, then closed the bottle and replaced it under the counter. He returned to the sink and added two inches of water to the glass, shut off the water, then turned off the pump switch.

"You've always got to remember to turn on the switches for the water—only thing different from ordinary plumbing—electrically operated pumps. I use several, so if one breaks down it won't kill all my water at once."

Rourke started out of the kitchen and back down the steps into the great room. Rubenstein was behind him. "John, this can't be real, I mean—"

"It is, Paul," Rourke said, turning. "It is. Go get cleaned up. Later I'll fix us something to eat."

"How about steak and eggs?" Rubenstein asked laughing.

Rourke didn't laugh. "Well, I'll have to flash thaw it, but I guess so. Powdered eggs all right?"

Rourke nursed his drink while Rubenstein showered. He got the steaks and set the microwave oven, then returned to the sofa. He was reading, not a book, but a catalogue of the books he had on the shelves along one wall of the great room—refreshing himself on the contents of his library—determining, now that it was his only library, if any gaps existed that critically needed filling. He put down the looseleaf binder and went to the bookshelves, rolled the ladder along their length and climbed up, selecting a book about projected climatalogical changes as the result of heat and temperature inversion. The red sunsets still worried him.

He heard Rubenstein behind him, turned and stepped down the ladder.

"All those books, John. What are these?" He stopped and pointed to a lower shelf.

"Just books I've written on weapons, survivalism, things like that. I've tried to have something of everything," Rourke said, sipping his drink and studying the cover of the book as if by holding it an answer to the bizarre climate would somehow come to him osmotically. "I always viewed a library as the most essential thing for survival beyond food, water, shelter, weapons. What good would it do if we survived, Paul, if all the wisdom of the world were lost to us? I may be misquoting but I believe it was Einstein who said that regardless of what World War Three was fought with—and I'm just paraphrasing—World War Four would be fought with rocks and clubs. Simply it means that civilization—

regardless of the physical reality of man—would end. It won't here." Rourke gestured broadly toward his books.

"Children's books too?" Rubenstein asked, looking at the lowest shelf.

"For Annie and Michael, perhaps their children someday. Can't teach them to read with these." Rourke gestured at the higher shelves. "Most of those children's books were illustrated or written and illustrated by Sarah, anyway—a double purpose."

"Do you really think it'll last that long?"

"The world or the aftermath of the War?" Rourke asked, turning away, not expecting an answer. He dropped the book on the coffee table, looked over his shoulder as he downed his drink, and said, "If the timer hits on the microwave, just push the off button. I'm taking a shower."

Rourke walked to the far side of the great room, past the waterfall, and up the three stone steps to the master bedroom. Curtains could be drawn to separate it from the rest of the retreat but he left them alone, going through his things to find a fresh change of clothes and dumping the contents of his pockets on top of the dresser. He went into the bathroom.

He shaved, brushed and flossed his teeth, then climbed into the shower, washing himself several times, washing his hair, and standing under the hot water. He then turned it to straight cold—from the underground spring the temperature was cold, very cold. Rourke, standing under the icy water, stared down at himself: a few cuts, a few bruises. He was intact, the last radiation reading on himself and his

58

equipment showed normalcy. He inhaled, able to count his ribs a little more easily, and he noticed too that more of the hair on his chest had turned to gray. He turned his face up to the spray, his eyes closed, feeling the water hammering on him, then shut off the water and stepped out to dry himself, shivering a little, unused still to the temperature of the cavern—a year-round constant 68 degrees because of the natural temperature of the rock and the water. It was a relief not to put on combat boots and wear instead a pair of rubber thongs.

Rourke couldn't see Rubenstein; he guessed the younger man was exploring. With his shirt tails out of his pants, his glass refilled and fresh cigar, Rourke walked toward the rear of the cavern, beyond the living quarters and shop area, past the waterfall. He stopped and smiled when he saw the look of bewilderment on Rubenstein's face.

"You're impressed?" Rourke asked, sipping at his drink.

"A greenhouse?" The younger man was staring at a small house of sheet plastic, humidity dripping from the windows, bright purple lights glowing from within.

"I wish I could use sunlight, but if I installed any sort of skylight, it would be visible from the air and that could blow the whole place. So, as long as the growlights hold out, we've got fresh vegetables, occasionally."

"I punched the off button on the microwave oven. You got everything here!"

"Not quite," Rourke said, then walked back in the kitchen.

The men ate, Rourke in relative silence. Rubenstein unending in his comments on the retreat. After dinner—time really didn't matter in any relative sense, Rourke realized—the two sat in the great room, drinking and talking. Rourke's watch read four A.M. for the outside world.

Rubenstein became tired and Rourke pointed him toward one of the spare bedrooms. He left Rourke alone in the great room. Rourke, unable to sleep, was still considering the note his wife had left and wondering where to begin the search. He found a videotape to his liking and put it on the machine. There was one of Sarah and the children, but he couldn't take seeing it, he told himself, so he watched a movie he'd recorded from commercial television two years earlier, he thought. It was a Western with the hero a gunfighting marshal up against a land baron. Rourke turned it off and found another tape, a science program on the big bang theory of the origins of the universe. He fixed another drink and watched the tape. Still wide awake when the tape ended, he found a movie more to his liking, a British secret agent after a top secret satellite. Rourke watched, fixed another drink, and wondered when the whiskey would run out.

Chapter 9

Natalia screamed again. Karamatsov pushed the bottle toward her. Inside herself, feelings of the guilt she held for betraying him by helping Rourke escape, the feelings for wanting to betray him and become Rourke's lover, the half-conscious, half-subconscious desire to be punished for doing what she knew to be wrong—these fought with her rationality. And against the pain. She could feel the lip of the bottle. She screamed again, knowing that somehow Karamatsov had won against her. She lashed out with her right arm, the knife edge of her hand slashing across her husband's Adam's apple, the heel of her left hand soaring up. Her body was acting independently of her will now, she realized, as though once the decision to defend herself had been made, a floodgate of vengeance and brutality had washed open. The heel of her left hand caught the tip of Vladmir's chin and hammered his head back.

Naked, she rolled to the floor, her husband fallen over the back of the couch.

He came at her, smiling, the belt in his hands, swinging it, but this time the side with the buckle.

She screamed at him, "Vladmir! Where are you?" And she realized the man she had virtually grown up with, married, loved, been faithful to except for one unconsummated indiscretion, was gone from her.

The brass belt buckle swung toward her and she dropped to the carpeted floor, sweeping her legs under his swing, against his legs, knocking him to the floor. The belt sailed from his hands as he fell. She threw herself on him, her knees hammering into his ribs and chest, her hand grasping for the tiny .38 Special revolver he carried, her right elbow jabbing into the side of his head as he fought to stop her.

She had the revolver. She cocked the hammer, the stubby muzzle less than an inch from his face, between his eyes. She didn't recognize her own voice. "I'll kill you if you move, bastard! Leave this house, leave me, leave us! I don't know you anymore. So help me, I'll shoot this thing between your eyes, and I'll laugh!"

Karamatsov stood up and she edged away from him. He threw up on the floor and stumbled toward the hall.

A long time after that, when he was gone, the door locked, she lowered her husband's gun and dropped to her knees and cried.

Chapter 10

John Thomas Rourke sat up, staring at the videotape on the television set. He realized immediately what had happened. The great room was dark; he'd fallen asleep watching the movie. And when he had recorded it, he'd left the tape running too long.

U.S. Navy jet fighters were soaring through the bright blue sky in perfect formation, the "Star Spangled Banner" was playing loudly. There were faces, too. A black child, an Hispanic farm laborer, a businessman, an Oriental woman, a housewife. The faces of children, men, women—Americans. The flag—fifty stars on a field of blue with thirteen stripes of red and white—it waved across the faces of the children. An American Eagle soared through the sky, the signoff cutting to the Washington Monument, the Lincoln Memorial, and an aerial view of the Statue of Liberty.

"And the home of the brave," Rourke stood up, knocking over the empty beer mug, tears welling up in his eyes in the darkness.

He fell to his knees as the flag waved in the wind, then suddenly the tape went blank. And the great room, inside a cavern, in a granite mountain, a retreat, bomb-hardened from anything except a direct hit of a nuclear device . . . Sarah, Michael, Ann—faces, Americans. Rourke wept in the darkness. It was all gone and perhaps only they survived all of it—the faces in memory.

Chapter 11

Sarah Rourke had kept the children riding after darkness had fallen—something she rarely did but the man at the farm hardened against brigand attack had not only known Millie Jenkins's Aunt Mary, but also known that brigand activity in the area was so intense that any stray traveler was likely to be killed—throat slit, possessions taken—forgotten, if anyone cared to forget. She kept the illegally modified AR-15 across her saddle horn—the safety on—but her trigger finger edged along the guard, ready.

Aunt Mary's last name was Molliner and the mention of the name had struck a responsive cord in Millie. The farm was high in the mountains and far from the Interstate Highway that had before the night of the war teemed with commercial and private vehicles. Sarah knew these mountains, or mountains like them, she thought. She had camped several times with John, especially before the children had been born. He had liked the mountains, telling her that they were strong and peaceful—like him, she now realized, yet like the mountains, capable of erupting in storms of violence when the conditions were right. And thunder was rumbling now in the higher peaks. There was little of the moon visible, except when a gust of wind would blow the purple tinged clouds from its face for a moment. She would use those moments to slow and look back at the children, study the trail. Was she going the right way? The man at the farmhouse had drawn a crude map for her, and so far all the landmarks he had cited had been easily found—but the way was so long, she thought. Had he purposely drawn a map to take her some long and remote route, she wondered, to avoid brigand contact?

She eased up in the saddle, her rear end hurting her. The wind gusted again, rain starting to fall light-ly. She started to turn, to say something to the children and, as she did, a gust of wind caught in a natural hedgerow to her right. She stared, thinking she'd seen some light beyond it.

She dismounted, holding Tildie's reins and snatch-ing at the reins of the children's horses. The rain started to pour down in sheets as she edged toward the bushes, pushing them aside as the wind lashed the rain against her with sudden, almost unimagin-able force. Water streaming down her eyes, the hair loosened from the bandanna plastered against her forehead, the T-shirt clinging to her body like a cold, wet, second skin, she saw light beyond the bushes. "A house," she muttered, then turned back toward

Michael. He was wearing a rain poncho she had cut for him from sheet plastic. He was riding Sam, her husband's black-stockinged, black-maned gray. "Michael, keep together—all of you—you in the lead behind me and the pack horse. If anything happens, Michael, get Annie and Millie out of here. Try to find that farmhouse where we stopped."

"What's the matter, Mom?" the six-year-old asked.

"I think I see a house—I'm not sure—it could be Millie's aunt's place. I'm not sure though."

She brushed the hair back from her forehead, squinting her eyelids shut against the rain. Michael hadn't let her down; he was his father's son, and she'd learned to rely on him. He had stabbed one of the men who had attacked the farm the morning after the night of the War, Michael had saved all their lives and saved her from—she shuddered at the memory. She had drunk the contaminated water. He had cared for her until her health had returned. She looked at him now, his wavy hair plastered by the rain to his head and face with the perfect upturned nose, the strong chin, the smiling eyes. "All right, Michael?"

"Okay," he said.

She wondered when this were ever through, could Michael go back to being a little boy again? She didn't think so: he had been a man too long now. Because of the rain, Sarah Rourke couldn't tell if there were tears welling up in her eyes.

She turned, handing back the reins of his horse to Michael, handing Millie the reins of the horse she rode with Annie, Annie half-asleep against the older girl's back despite the rain and rough country. Sarah hauled herself wearily into the wet saddle, bending across and shaking Annie, then snatching the little girl into her arms across the saddle horn, displacing the AR-15. She handed the rifle to Michael. "The safety's on; don't touch it, Michael!" Managing the reins of Tildie and the Jenkins's horse used as a pack animal, her daughter Annie in her arms, Sarah started forward around the hedgerow and toward the light.

A broad, open field lay beyond, rocky and with high grass, the wind whipping the sodden grass against her legs and the horses, the rain so heavy now Sarah could barely see beyond the horse she rode. But the light was still there—that she could still make out. The wind was blowing harder now, driving the rain against her. She glanced behind her again and again to make certain none of the children had fallen behind. She felt her horse stumbling, the animal starting to go down. She slid from the wet saddle, Annie clutched against her breast. The ground was hard despite the rain, the grass lashing at her face as she forced herself to her knees. She glanced back to Michael and shouted, "No, I'm all right! Stay mounted and keep an eye on Millie!"

Sarah Rourke, her body wet and aching, her arms stiff from holding her daughter against her, pushed herself to her feet and caught up the reins of her own horse and the pack horse, then stared at the yellow light beyond the end of the field. She started walking toward it, the rain hammering against her, obscuring her vision. She would turn her face away from it, then glance back toward it at an angle so she could see for a few seconds before the rain blurred her vision again. She could tell now that the yellow light was from a farmhouse window.

She stumbled to one knee, pushed herself up, and walked on, holding the sleeping Annie in her arms, the reins to the two horses tight in her left fist, the animals balking. She was tired—a mother, a mother to the children of her body, a mother now to the orphaned Millie Jenkins since her parents had been killed. Sarah Rourke laughed, swallowing too much of the rain, choking for an instant. She was a mother even to the horses. She could hear herself as if the voice belonged to someone else, cajoling the animals, telling them to be good, to walk just a little farther in the darkness and rain. Sarah Rourke, mother and adventurer, she thought. She laughed.

The farmhouse loomed ahead of her in a massive shadow, the yellow light brighter and clearly visible from a side window.

She stumbled once again, this time banging her elbows hard on the ground as she fought to keep her weight from crushing her four-year-old daughter. She got to her knees, leaned back on her heels, then one leg at a time, stood, then started forward, glancing behind her to the children, talking low and soft to the animals. The rain washed over her body and her body racked with chills.

The house was twenty yards ahead, she judged, and she quickened her pace. She saw the window clearly, a small porch and side door near it. She stopped at the base of the low steps, forced one leg, then the other, then again and again, and she was standing, swaying on the porch.

She kicked at the door and the door opened. A young man with a shotgun in his hands stood framed in the blinding yellow light from the kitchen beyond, a woman in a house dress standing behind him.

Sarah Rourke gasped, "Aunt Mary, I brought you Millie Jenkins."

There was heat from the kitchen, and the warm dry air made her start to feel faint.

She heard a woman's voice shout, "Get out of my way! Her baby!"

Sarah started to fall forward, felt a man's rough hands catch at her and Annie swept from her arms as she sank to her knees.

Chapter 12

Rourke sat at the kitchen counter, staring into the empty great room, sipping at his own strong black coffee. He had arisen early, Rourke time of eleven A.M. He had cleaned the guns, including Rubenstein's High Power and MP-40, then performed the necessary maintenance on the liberated Harley Low Rider, and checked his own machine.

He had showered and changed. Next he had gotten out the Lowe Alpine Systems Loco pack, the kind used by search and rescue teams—to Rourke's thinking the perfect all-around pack with an integral frame. He had put off loading it, being hungry. He stared at the waterfall and the pool, wondering what Sarah and the children would say when they first saw the retreat—if they ever would see it. He scratched the last thought; he would find them and bring them back—bring them home. They *would* see it. He imagined the children playing in the shallow pool beneath the falls.

He poured another cup of coffee, working with pencil and paper to list what he would bring. He would leave soon to scout the area for Soviet and brigand activity and pick up the trail of Sarah and the children. He noted down items on the list: both of the Detonics pistols, the small Musette bag with spare magazines and ammo, the Bushnell 8 x 30 armored binoculars, the big, handmade Chris Miller Bowie knife. He stopped and looked up. Rubenstein entered the great room from the side bedroom where he'd been sleeping.

"Hello, Paul, you trying for an endurance record?" Rourke glanced at his Rolex. Rubenstein had retired fourteen hours earlier.

"The first time I figured somebody wasn't going to shoot me in the middle of the night or something. Sorry."

"No need to be. Have some coffee." Rourke answered. Rubenstein ascended the three stone steps into the kitchen. "There's orange juice in the refrigerator. Just look around and fix yourself some breakfast."

"Orange juice?" Rubenstein asked, his eyes wide behind his glasses.

"Yeah—frozen from concentrate." Rourke thought of something else to add to the list: one of the Harry Owens barrel inserts for the Detonics so he could fire .22 rimfires if he potted a rabbit or something.

"John?" Rubenstein began.

"I don't know when I'm leaving—soon, though, but I won't be out long this first trip, so you just take it easy."

"My parents—I want to go down to St. Petersburg, see if there still is a St. Petersburg, see if they're alive."

"I know," Rourke said, then smiled at the younger man standing across the counter from where Rourke sat. "I'll miss you, Paul. I'll always count you my best friend—"

"Listen, if, ahh—" Rubenstein stammered.

"Take whatever you need to get there and stay alive. I've got plenty and I can get more."

"No, I didn't—I mean, if they're dead, would you—"

"My home—" Rourke gestured to the cavern walls and ceiling—"is your home—*mi casa es su casa, amigo*. Yeah, I'd like it if things work out that way. And for your sake I hope they don't, but I'd like it if you came back. I could use your help finding Sarah and the children; the kids could use an uncle."

"John, I—"

"Don't. You can't leave for a while, remember, I'm a doctor? You need about a week of rest before those wounds will be healed enough for you to travel hard. I want to teach you a few things before you go anyway: couple of tricks that might help you stay alive. Give you a few things—a good knife, some maps, a good compass, show you how to use it—show you how to take care of your bike. You know some of that already anyway."

"John, do you think you're going to find them—Sarah and the children, I mean?" Rubenstein asked, sipping a mug of coffee.

"Yeah, I've thought about it. And, yeah, I'll find them, no matter what. See—" and Rourke stood up, poured himself another cup of coffee, then leaned against the counter, staring past Rubenstein toward the great room—"see, we never had much time to talk, you and I. I think Natalia always wondered about that, what makes me tick? I decided years ago, back in Latin America that time I had to stay alive on my own after the CIA team I was with got ambushed and I was wounded. The thing that makes one person stay alive no matter what and another person buy it—there's some luck to it, sure. The toughest man or woman on earth can be at ground zero of a nuclear blast and he's going to die. But under general conditions, what makes one person survive and another lose is—well, there're a lot of names for it. Some people call it meanness, some call it tenaciousness—whatever. But it's will—you will yourself not to die, not to give up. Nobody out there's going to kill me," Rourke said, gesturing toward the steel doors leading into the entrance hall and the outside world beyond. "Nobody out there's going to kill me or stop me—unless I let them do it. Sure, somebody could be up in the rocks and blow the back of my head open with a sniper rifle, and you can't control that—but in a situation, a conflict—" Rourke struggled for the right words—"it's not that I'm any better or tougher or smarter. I just won't quit. You know what I mean, Paul? It's hard to explain, really."

"I know—I've seen that in you," Rubenstein said.

"Yeah, you want to teach me that?"

"I couldn't if I wanted to—and I don't need to.

You just need to sharpen a few more of the skills that'll let you stay alive. You've got will enough already. I don't worry about you out there anymore than I worry about myself. You're a good man. I haven't said that to very many people," Rourke concluded, then stared back at his list, sipping his coffee, aware of the sounds of Rubenstein making himself breakfast, aware of the sounds of the water from the falls, then the water crashing down into the pool.

He wrote something on the list—the one item that made his skin crawl because it represented something he couldn't combat head-to-head: "Geiger counter." He swallowed his coffee and almost burned his mouth.

Chapter 13

Varakov stared out from the balcony again, at the
skeletons of the mastodons. Karamatsov said he had
slipped when Varakov asked him earlier that morning about the bruises on the right side of his face.
And Natalia, Karamatsov had said, was feeling ill
and might not be in for several days. Varakov had
dispatched Vladmir Karamatsov to the southeast, to
aid Colonel Korcinski in setting up the new military
district. There was a tough Resistance movement
forming in the area, intelligence reports indicated.

Ever since the business in Texas, Varakov had
realized that Natalia had betrayed Karamatsov
somehow, and that Karamatsov was not quite right
in the head anymore, perhaps because of it. The
aftermath of the debacle and the loss of Samuel
Chambers had shown a ruthlessness in Karamatsov
that Varakov had always suspected, but never imagined in its scope. He had executed several of his own

men for allowing the escape; he had used his forces to kill every suspected member of the Texas militia—a bloodbath Varakov had not seen the likes of since the purges of the thirties under Stalin.

A soldier's stock in trade was bloodletting, but there was a difference between warfare and murder. Karamatsov was a murderer, pure and simple, Varakov thought. And the thought made him wonder all the more about Natalia. Had something happened?

Varakov leaned over the railing, calling out to his secretary below, "Cancel my appointments for this afternoon. Call up my car and driver. I have business to attend to. If something must be signed and you think it should be signed, then forge my name. Hurry."

He trusted the girl; that was part of being a human being, he had always thought, trusting those who deserved trust and distrusting those who would stab you in the back and smile over your still warm body. He distrusted Karamatsov for exactly that reason, and he found his palms sweating as he started down the low, broad steps from the mezzanine overlooking the main gallery. He was worried about Natalia, the beautiful Natalia, the superlative agent, the tough fighter, the gentle girl—his dead brother's only daughter.

Chapter 14

Sarah Rourke sat up in bed, startled, then a smile crossed her lips as the strong sunlight bathed her face in its warmth. She remembered the previous night. After her collapse on the kitchen floor, she had revived, finding that Mary Mulliner had fed, bathed, and bedded not only her niece Millie, but Michael and Annie as well. Mary Mulliner had offered Sarah a home for as long as she had wanted it. Sarah smiled, throwing back the sheet, and stared at her feet. She wiggled her toes and stood up, and the borrowed yellow nightgown fell to the floor past her ankles. Slippers were beside the bed, but she didn't remember them from the previous night. She stepped into them, walked across the small bedroom of the country farmhouse to the full length mirror on the inside of the door. She looked at herself. She had showered and washed her hair before going to bed. She ran her hands through her hair now, letting it fall to her shoulders. She turned around, staring at her unfamiliar image. She had not worn anything besides jeans in—she couldn't remember how long and was too happy to try.

There was a long robe across the bottom of the bed, yellow like the nightgown, and she put it on, belted it around her waist. She realized for the first time that she had lost weight these many weeks since the night of the war. She walked to the door, opened it, and stepped into a hallway. A staircase was at the end—she remembered that—and she started toward it, then stopped as she passed a half-open doorway. Michael and Annie were sleeping in a huge double bed, sunlight streaming across it. Annie was not sucking her thumb, for a change, and Michael peaceful and smiling, rolled over, stretched and hunched down against his pillow.

Sarah leaned against the doorframe and stared at the sunlight. The wind through the slightly open window blew the white curtain wildly. "Thank you," she said if anyone were listening. She wanted to see the outside, and turned and ran down the stairs, almost tripping in the unfamiliar slippers and the floor-length gown. She saw Mary Mulliner in the living room, but passed her, and went to the front door, opened it, and ran onto the porch. The sky—the sky—there was a breeze blowing, a dog barking and, for the first time in weeks, that sound didn't terrify her. She stared up at the sky and heard herself laughing, threw her head back, her arms outstretched. It was as if there were some beautiful music playing, she thought, then she stopped laughing, turned and saw Mary Mulliner and her teenage son staring at her, standing behind her on the porch. The older woman just said, "I understand you—least I think I do, Sarah."

Sarah Rourke turned to the woman and hugged her.

Chapter 15

Varakov sat in the back seat of his staff car, a Lincoln Continental expropriated from a parking lot near what had been the United States Federal Building in downtown Chicago. There had been, he reflected, that one more urgent reason for sending Vladmir Karamatsov to the southeast, more urgent he felt than the brigands and the Resistance.

After Texas, Karamatsov had moved directly to Florida, working through Cuban liaisons to determine what the exact nature of the launches at Cape Canaveral from the space center there had been the night of the war.

All the missiles the U.S. had launched, Varakov understood, had been accounted for. These launches were the only exceptions and that worried Kremlin leadership. It worried Varakov because it hinted that somehow the Americans had prepared for the possibility of war and, despite the crushing losses, perhaps had some new weapon no one had dreamed of—up in space now perhaps. He stared up at the gray Chicago sky through his back seat window. He wondered. During the exchanges, each side's hunter-killer satellites had destroyed spy satellites of the other side. Nothing remained in orbit except the hunter-killers and the Soviet space platform—which was now useless, Varakov thought, since the Soviet Union had no time, money, or desire to explore the reaches of space—surviving after the war would take all the efforts the people of the Soviet Union could muster.

If the Americans had put some mysterious weapons system in orbit, there remained no way of detecting it. The Soviet manned platform was in a polar orbit, and all the Americans would have needed to do was place their vehicles in an orbit out of range of the platform, perhaps around the South Pole regions. He was not an astronomer or a missile scientist; he didn't know nor could he guess. He thought that perhaps it was some doomsday device, placed in orbit to detonate after a specific period of time if some radio signal were not received to scrub the mission—some gigantic burst that would blow away the atmosphere, the final retribution for the Soviet attack. The thought unsettled him. He had survived much, always because he had willed himself to do so—this he could not impose his will against. There had been a mysterious reference found in a looseleaf notebook in an Air Force Intelligence installation: the words "Eden Project" and the drawing of an upward vectoring rocket ship beside it. Nothing else. Varakov wondered if the words Eden

Project and the mysterious multiple launchings from Cape Canaveral were related. This was Karamatsov's prime and secret reason for being in the southeast.

Intelligence also indicated that apparently one official of the National Aeronautics and Space Administrations—NASA—survived, an official with the level of responsibility that he might know what exactly had been launched that night. He was a chief public information officer for NASA, the name in the file had been James R. Colfax. Varakov recalled the man had been an astronaut, then moved into administration with NASA after a heart condition had disqualified him for space flight. He had piloted one of the space shuttles the Americans had been so proud of. This Colfax, Varakov thought, he would know.

He had been making a speaking tour, recruiting for NASA at the time of the war and had a home somewhere in Georgia in the mountains. If he would be anywhere he could be "officially" found, he would be there, Varakov had reasoned. People and animals were of little difference. A wounded animal goes to its burrow or nest or cave; a man whose world is destroyed goes to his home—it was the same.

And, according to intelligence files, the man Varakov knew had defeated Karamatsov—John Rourke—had his home in Georgia as well. If Rourke had survived after the affair in Texas, he might be there by now. It was food for Karamatsov's ego to have suffered defeat at the hands of an American—and perhaps the two men would cross each other's paths again.

Varakov's driver pulled up to the white painted brick house in the expensive suburb, the house where Karamatsov and Natalia lived.

"Stop here. I will walk up the driveway. Stay in the car. I will get my door," Varakov said, scrunching his feet into his shoes, wrapping his great coat closed around him and stepping out onto the concrete driveway. He had not called. He had not taken a helicopter in order to call as little attention to this personal business as he could.

He was cold. The weather in America was insane, he decided. It had been hot three days earlier. He walked toward the low steps, then mounted them heavily, and stood by the door. He rang the doorbell and waited. He rang the doorbell again; thinking then that perhaps it was out of order, he knocked his gloved right fist against the white wooden door, not bothering with the brass doorknocker.

There was no answer. "Natalia!" he shouted.

Again there was no answer. "You are home—I know that—answer the door. It is an order."

There was no answer and as he began to speak he could hear her voice from beyond the door. "Please—I am sick—I can see no one."

"Let me in—now!"

"No, I'm going upstairs, please leave." And the voice stopped.

His thick lips twisted downward. He stomped down the steps toward the car and his driver. The man started from the car and Varakov waved him back. "My briefcase—give it to me—now." He took the case through the open window, set it roughly on the hood of the Lincoln, spun the combination and opened the lock, then took a battered 9mm PM from the case, slammed the case closed and spun the tumblers. "Put it away," he commanded without looking at the driver.

Varakov strode up the driveway, his feet not hurting him, drawing the slide back on the Makarov and chambering a round, leaving the hammer back as he mounted the steps.

"If you are near the door, stand away!" There was no answer. He took a step back and fired the pistol once, then again into the mechanism of the lock, then threw his shoulder against it. The door sprang inward. He regained his balance, then manually lowered the hammer on the Makarov and pushed up the safety lever, dropping the pistol in the pocket of his great coat. With his hamlike left fist he punched the door closed behind him. He stood in the vestibule, looking down into the living room and shouted, "Natalia!"

"Uncle." He turned and saw her standing by a swinging door leading from the opposite end of the living room, he assumed into the kitchen. Women spent a great deal of time in kitchens even when they weren't cooking. It was like a man and his office, Varakov thought.

He stopped thinking when he saw her face. She wore heavy makeup, and she usually wore little or none. Despite the makeup, he could see the darkness of bruises. He stepped down into the living room, stared at the dark stain in the white carpet, then saw tiny red stains on the couch.

"You and Vladmir—you fought—he beat you."

"He told—" and she seemed to catch herself.

"No, he told me nothing. Come here to me, child." He reached out his arms. Natalia ran toward him and sank her head against his massive chest. His arms went around her. She was crying. He stroked her back and she winced. He pushed her away.

"Let me see your body."

She took a step back. He studied her. She wore a long sleeved white blouse, buttoned high at the neck, a black skirt extending to the middle of her calves, and low-heeled black shoes. He repeated himself, "Let me see your body, child. I changed your diapers when you were a baby; I bathed you once. I am your father's brother. You should not fear my eyes. Either remove your blouse so I may see your back or I will call to my chauffeur and have him use the radio to send two women here to undress you—six women if I need it—let me see your back."

Varakov watched her dark eyes, watched her long fingers move slowly to the buttons at her collar, watched her slip the bow there, then slip each of the pearl-looking buttons through the button holes. She left the cuffs of the blouse closed, pulling the blouse from her skirt, letting it drop behind her, her arms limp at her sides. She wore a slip that covered her abdomen and much of her back.

"Turn around."

Natalia obeyed. He could see the trailing edge of red welts above the lace forming the upper portion of the slip against her back. He took a step closer to her, both his hands grabbing the slip, then ripping it down the back. He stripped away his right glove and undid the back of her bra. He saw her hands raising to her chest.

86

"I need to see no more, child," Varakov said slowly, studying the dozen or more welts across her back.

"He beat you with a belt. Is the rest of your body like this?"

He looked at her face in profile over her left shoulder, her eyes cast down. He watched her nod.

"What else did he do?" Varakov asked, forcing his voice to remain even and sound calm and fatherly.

"He—" Her voice faltered, and she turned toward him, her hands still holding her clothes against her breasts, her face against his chest. He knew what she was going to say, but couldn't. When he was young, a husband raping his wife was a logical absurdity. If a man wanted his wife and she did not want him, that was her misfortune. Things were different these days, he thought, and the thought didn't distress him.

"I know, Natalia. Why? It is none of my business, but why?"

"The man, Rourke—I cannot—"

"I am your uncle, not your commanding officer. I don't care. Tell me."

She looked up into his eyes. Her eyes were sad like they had been when her father—his brother—had died. "I fell in love with . . . with Rourke. But nothing happened between us. He saved my life, I had to save him, it was my honor to do this." Varakov loved his native language at times, and her soft contralto gave it the beauty it deserved.

"You should remember the first duty of a soldier, Natalia, child—duty is ranked before honor—and honor is often a luxury. But I respect honor. Tell me.'' And he looked into her eyes again.

"What, Uncle?"

"Would you go back to Vladmir?"

"He only punished me as I deserved to be punished.''

"You are not only beautiful, but you are naive. Punishment is in the soul. The body is not punished; it is given pain. A man beats a woman—'' he sighed heavily— "a man hits a woman perhaps in anger, once, perhaps twice—perhaps that is just. A man beats a woman not to punish her, but to expiate himself, child. He did not do this to you because of something in you, but because of something in him. And I was afraid you would say such foolishness that you would return to him.''

He said nothing else, just sat down with her on the couch and listened to her cry, listened to her tell him very slowly what had happened, sat quietly and thought while she changed clothes, then stayed to the early hours of the morning with her, lingering over a dinner she made for him as she had many times when she was a child. They talked about her father, about trips to the Black Sea resort they had loved, about her marriage to Karamatsov.

He left after drinking too much; his chauffeur was almost visibly angry at the late hour. As Varakov sat back in his seat, his great coat huddled around him, he softly verbalized two thoughts. "She is a sincere cook, but not a gifted one; I will cause Karamatsov somehow to die.''

Chapter 16

"Comrade General!"

Varakov opened his eyes. He heard gunfire, the hum of the engine was louder than it should have been. He looked out the window, startled. The area he recognized from his initial tour of the city was the portion of the city that had been all but destroyed in racial riots many years back in the 1960s. And now there was gunfire all around him.

"What is it?" he asked, but he already knew: the freedom fighters, the people who had survived by being far enough away from the neutron bombs, the people who lived in basements and hidden bomb shelters, who carried guns, killed Russian soldiers, and threw crude gasoline bombs at Soviet vehicles; they called them—the nerve—Molotov cocktails.

No sooner had the thought left his mind than it returned, the shattering of a glass bottle in the street beside them and the roar of an explosion, a fireball, the car swerving to the side.

"Get out of here now, Leon, and you get two weeks leave in Moscow and a letter to a brothel a woman I know keeps." He smiled. Leon was the best driver to be had and would get him out of there anyway—if it could be done. Varakov drew the pistol from his greatcoat pocket where he'd left it, pushed the button for his window to roll down, then fired into the street. He saw figures running, their shadows made larger than life by the flickering of the flames, a Soviet truck overturned and burning.

He almost lost the gun outside the window as Leon, his driver, wheeled the Lincoln around a corner and onto a highway feeder ramp. "We are going in the wrong direction, Comrade General Varakov."

"It does not matter, Leon," he rasped across the seat back separating them.

"Get down!" the driver shouted and Varakov knew better than not to obey. Rocks and bricks pelted at them from a walking bridge over the expressway, the windshield shattering and the car careening toward a guard rail. Varakov dropped to the floor, felt the bounce and lurch, the jerkiness of the car's movements, then the shudder as the car stopped.

With the pistol in his hands, he rose from his knees and pried open the door on the driver's side. He could hear sirens in the distance. They were Russian, he knew. He saw a figure fleeing across the walking bridge, raised his pistol and lowered it without firing. Then Varakov looked down to Leon. The boy's face was halfway through the windshield and one of the eyes was bulged out. It seemed that the head had almost exploded.

He closed his eyes and asked himself out loud, "If all those fools so believe in you, God—why this?" He realized as he walked from the car toward the advancing military police vehicles the mere fact the clouds had not parted and no voice had rumbled like thunder and answered him proved nothing—at least he secretly hoped that.

Chapter 17

Rourke revved the jet-black Harley-Davidson Low Rider and glided the machine onto the highway. Traveling on the road was dangerous, he knew, because the Russians might be patrolling it. The wind whipped at his face—cold wind because, again, the temperature had begun to change. He shivered slightly inside the waist-length leather jacket. He stopped the bike, easing over to the shoulder, years of driving habit still forcing him to automatically glance over his shoulder along the deserted road, to work his signal flasher.

He had seen the signs of a large vehicular force on some of the side roads since he had left the retreat at dawn that morning—brigands, he suspected. He lit a cigar, the blue yellow flame of his battered Zippo flickering in the wind.

Rourke had told Paul Rubenstein he would be back within four days or less, but experience had taught Rourke to prepare for three times that period. The Lowe Alpine Loco pack was strapped to the back of the Harley with food, medical supplies, clothing—all the necessities. Two straps crossed his chest: on his left side hung the musette bag with some of his spare ammo and a few packages of dehydrated fruit that he'd made himself with the Equi-Flow dehydrator he kept at the retreat. On the right hung the binoculars—the armored Bushnells. Beneath these in a Ranger leather camouflage holster similar to the one he used for the Python was his Colt Government MK IV series '70 .45, Metalifed with the Colt Medallion Pachmayr grips and the Detonics competition recoil system installed. The twin Detonics stainless pistols hung in the double Alessi rig under his arms.

The gunbelt around his waist carried spare Colt magazines for the government and these also doubled with the Detonics pistols. From the left side of the belt hung a bayonet for the M-16. It fit the CAR-15 slung across Rourke's back, muzzle down, muzzle cap off, thirty-round magazine inserted.

He squinted against the sun despite the aviator sunglasses he wore. There was an expressway exit ramp ahead and he detected smoke, he thought, rising from the road near it. He mounted the Harley again and swung onto the road, leaning back and letting the machine out.

It took Rourke less than three minutes at eighty-five to reach the ramp and begin to slow for it, then turn up on the cross road and cut to the far side of the Interstate Highway toward the smoke—it was a gasoline station, burning, several abandoned cars in the lot—a disgruntled customer, Rourke thought, smiling. He doubted there had been any gasoline in the underground tanks for weeks or any electrical power to pump it. He stopped the bike, dismounting, sliding the Colt CAR-15 on its sling from his back to under his right arm, his left hand sweeping back the bolt and letting it fly forward, chambering a round. His right fist locked on the pistol grip, his trigger finger along the edge of the guard, the safety off.

He saw something in a smashed and battered four-door sedan near the flames of the burning gas station building. He walked slowly toward it, the cigar clamped in his teeth in the left corner of his mouth. He stopped. It was a partially decomposed, partially eaten human skeleton. He moved closer to it. The top of the skull was split wide in the back—a blow, he guessed, from a large, not-so-blunt instrument, maybe a jack handle. He wondered who the man had been, then wheeled, hearing a low growl.

He edged closer to the car. Six dogs, two of them slavering and foaming, all of them huge German Shepherd-size or larger, tongues hanging out, saliva dripping from their mouths. He'd encountered feral dogs before—and rabid dogs. These were. In a few days, the ones foaming at the mouth would be dead, the others would follow shortly. If he were even scratched by one of them, he would have perhaps a few days at most to find rabies vaccine or die like them—mad.

His jaw set, he licked his lower lip. He distrusted the light, fast, penetrating .223 solids on dogs. Even if he shot one of the dogs through, it could still come down on him, bite him, scratch him, knock him down so the other dogs could swarm over him.

He needed the .45—six dogs, only six rounds in each of the Detonics pistols, but there were seven in the Colt. He always fed the chambered round from the magazine, leaving the magazine one round down so the round would be edged forward for more reliable feeding.

Seven 185-grain JHPs in the Colt, six dogs. He gave a mental shrug as one of the dogs edged toward him. He loosed his right hand grip on the CAR-15 and snatched for the Colt on his hip, his thumb breaking the snap on the flap, the gun snaking up, his thumb wiping down the safety catch of the Colt, his first finger starting the squeeze as the muzzle lined up on the nearest of the wild dogs, its mouth spraying foam as it leaped toward him. Rourke fired. His bullet caught the animal in the throat and he jumped to the left, firing again at a second dog—he couldn't tell what kind other than big. It was turning, starting to jump. His second round nailed the animal in the chest and it dropped.

He fired. Some of the dogs were now starting to run, but they were rabid and he had to stop them. The third dog took two rounds as it leaped toward him, two rounds before it fell. He shot his fifth round into the fourth dog, dropping it. The last two weren't interested in him anymore and were running. Rourke dropped to his right knee, fired his sixth round at the fifth dog, then, both hands bracing the Metalifed Colt auto, he fired his last round—the last of the fleeing dogs bounded on a few yards, then keeled over in mid-stride.

Rourke stood up and breathed hard. Swapping magazines, he thumbed down the slide stop and left the safety off as he walked from animal to animal, verifying they were dead.

He holstered the gun, having upped the safety, then looked back at the half-eaten skeleton in the car. He knew now what had half-eaten it.

He found rags and made a torch, lit them from the licking flames of the gas station office and tossed the rags into the car seat to dispose of the dead man. The rabid dogs should be burned or buried to prevent the spread of infection, he thought. Cursing softly, he went back to the Harley, got his gloves and his trench shovel and started up the shoulder of the road, looking for a soft spot.

Digging the grave and hauling the six dead animals had consumed forty-five minutes, he noted, as he wiped off the blade of the trench shovel and strapped it with his pack on the back of the bike. "Dammit," Rourke muttered half-aloud. He stowed the gloves in his pack and remounted his cycle. He had not wasted the time spent digging the mass grave for the rabid animals. He turned the Harley down the road leading from the Interstate. The fire had probably been set—that meant brigands, and Rourke wanted an idea of their strength. He started up toward the mountains again.

When Rourke stopped once more, his watch and the sunlight agreed—it was approximately three o'clock: the wind was stronger and the temperature getting cooler. He had left the highway—a two-lane road—and turned off onto dirt and followed this along toward a valley. Lying on his belly, he stared into the valley now, his eyes tight against the binoculars, the objective lenses sweeping the town in the valley floor. There was one main street, and at its end by the edge of the town was a large, wide grave. For two people, he thought. In the town, standing around a long abandoned pickup truck were more than a dozen men and women, their vehicles parked at the opposite end of the street—an assortment of pickup trucks, several motorcycles of varying quality and one badly damaged station wagon.

More of the brigands waited by the vehicles: Rourke guessed there were thirty of them in the valley all told. He edged along the lip of the valley, getting back into tree cover to avoid detection; he was concerned they might have someone exploring the rim of the valley.

Still able to see into the town, though his field of view was reduced, Rourke waited for more than fifteen minutes, observing through the Bushnells— finally, the knot of brigand men and women broke up around the abandoned pickup truck and they started back toward the vehicles and the rest of their number back at the other side of the town. Rourke didn't smile. He planned to slip down into the town; the large grave bore investigation, he thought.

It was another ten minutes before the last of the brigand vehicles disappeared in the distance, then Rourke waited another five minutes. Patience was something he knew he could never sacrifice. Swinging the CAR-15 into position—slung now just under his right arm suspended from his right shoulder—the chamber still loaded, the safety on, he slipped down along the side of the valley, past pine trees, guiding around through bushes. He skidded the last few feet to the valley floor on the dirt and gravel, dropping into a low crouch, the muzzle of the CAR-15 sweeping from one side of the street to the other. Standing—the safety off, his finger near the trigger—he edged forward, the scoped rifle's stock collapsed, his left hand free.

Spent cartridge casings littered the ground and where there was dirt rather than paving, the cartridges were half buried. From the corrosion and the depth to which the cartridges were covered with dirt, he judged there had been a large scale, prolonged gunfight there—but several weeks earlier. There were picked clean bones in the street, some of the skeletons still partially clad with rotting clothing, but all this with rips and tears. He stopped at one body, looking through the shredded shirt and the bare bleached rib cage. There was a tarnished police badge on the ground. Rourke looked at the empty eye sockets in the skull. The skull was punctured by what Rourke judged as .45 ACP Slugs. The man had apparently died doing his duty trying to defend his town. Rourke scanned the ground, found a half-fallen-down wooden sign, ripped it down the rest of the way, and dragged it back, laying it over the top half of the dead police officer. He kept walking. There were more cartridge cases, some plastic shotshell cases, a rusted and bent-out-of-shape magazine for some pistol he couldn't immediately identify.

He walked back through the town then, going up to the grave, which was unmarked. He wondered, debating whether to go back up to the bike and get his shovel. He started to turn toward the near side of the valley, to climb back toward where he'd hidden the bike, but stopped. There were motors rumbling in the distance and he saw the grille of a pickup truck turning down the street into the town. Rourke ran, his lips drawn back from his teeth, toward the closest edge of the valley. He half dove into the brush, then dropped: the brigands were returning. He couldn't afford to be trapped in the valley. He started up the slope. His bike was in the other direction, but he could circle to get it. Rourke reached the rim of the valley, sinking to the ground from the uphill deadrun.

The brigands were returning in force. He mentally noted to return and check the gravesite later. He started off through the brush again, circling wide along the rim of the valley toward the Harley. He heard a noise, dropped into a crouch near some bushes and waited. The noise did not repeat itself, and he dismissed it, but stared at the ground.

He took the bayonet from his belt—the Bowie knife was in his pack—and scratched at the ground with the tip of the blade. It was a foil packet from some of the food similar to what he had left for Sarah, buried but partially uncovered. Some animal had probably scented it, begun to dig it out then, but been frightened off. In the corner of the package was a black ink date stamp—he stamped all his food with the date of acquisition.

"Sarah," he thought, muttering the name out loud. He moved along the ground on his hands and knees, searching for some further clue he hoped to find. He stopped again. More of the food packages—and a footprint. He dropped back on his haunches, leaned against a tree trunk, and his face broadened with a smile. "Annie," he sighed. He took off the sunglasses and stared at the footprint, faint but clear. With the tip of the bayonet blade he deepened the lines of the footprint—a child's tennis shoe with a design in the center. He remembered when he'd been with Sarah and the children prior to leaving for Canada, a few days before the night of the war. Annie had proudly made him look at the soles of her new tennis shoes: there was a daisy, a raised yellow daisy in the center of each sole. As he scratched the ground with the point of the bayonet, he drew out the design of a flower— a daisy. "Annie!" He walked the area, uncaring about the brigands in the valley below. There were the remains of several fires, branches to which he could tell horses had been tied. They had camped there, were traveling by horseback and, from the branch markings, he judged, there were three or four horses—Tildie, Sarah's mare and Sam, his own horse—and at least one, possibly two other horses. He sat down on the ground. The Jenkins family had lived nearby, he remembered suddenly; they rode. Mr. Jenkins—Rourke couldn't remember his first name—had been in the Army or Marine Corps, Rourke couldn't remember which. A retired non-com, Rourke recalled. If Sarah and the children were with Jenkins and his wife—didn't they have a daughter, he tried remembering?

Rourke realized too that if this had been their camp—and he was sure it had—they were likely miles away, but on horseback the mileage they could cover was nothing compared to what he could cover on the Harley.

He got to his feet, searching the camp area in greater detail, the light starting slowly to fade now, the wind picking up again. He could tell nothing of the direction in which they had gone, but he guessed the mountains. On a hunch, he decided to head north. If the mountains were thought safe, then the deeper in the mountains, the safer. He took off at a run for the Harley, checking on the brigands in the town down in the valley once more, then emptied the chamber of the CAR-15 and mounted up.

"Tennessee," he said half-aloud, starting the bike between his legs. With horses they would be lucky to make twenty miles in a day—especially with the children—there would have to be other campsites, telltale leavings of food, footprints. He wondered if there would be more cartridge cases, forcing himself not to consider what could lie in the large grave at the edge of the town.

Chapter 18

Rourke skidded the Harley to a stop. In the half-light as darkness was laying long shadows from the tall pines across the ground he had almost missed them, six men, armed, wearing camouflage clothing and moving in rapid dog trot across the clearing.

Rourke started for the Detonics .45 under his left arm, his nearest gun, wrestling the bike to the left with his left hand, the stainless Detonics coming into his hand, his thumb drawing back the semi-spurless hammer, the muzzle snaking forward to fire, his left hand free of the bike already reaching for the second of the two pistols under his right armpit.

"Rourke! Is that you?"

Rourke stopped his left hand, his right arm fully extended, his finger against the trigger. "Rourke? John Rourke?"

Rourke lowered the Detonics in his right fist, but only slightly, not quite recognizing the voice, but knowing it sounded familiar. "John Rourke!" the voice repeated.

Rourke stepped off the Harley, balancing it on the stand, the gun hanging at his right side, the hammer still cocked, his finger beside the trigger guard. He started toward the tallest of the six camouflaged figures, the man speaking. He recognized the voice now.

"Reed? Captain Reed?"

"Yes. John Rourke! God, what a sight for sore eyes, man!"

Rourke hated that expression: "a sight for sore eyes." If it made your eyes sore, he'd always thought then why want to see it? And if your eyes were sore to begin with, seeing something however welcome would do little to make them less sore. He realized as he walked toward Reed, that among his many credits before the war had not been a famous sense of humor.

"Captain Reed," Rourke said softly, realizing he still had the gun in his right hand. He upped the safety and switched it to his left hand, and took Reed's offered hand.

"Rourke, we got airdropped in here last night. I kept hoping somehow we'd bump into you, man."

"Well," Rourke said, glancing over his shoulder around the clearing, "if we keep standing around out here in the open, we won't be air dropped, we'll be dropped. Come on." And without waiting for Reed, Rourke turned, walked across the clearing in broad strides, lowering the safety then lowering the hammer on the Detonics, reholstering it under his jacket as he approached the Harley. He climbed on the bike, saying over his shoulder, "I'll meet you over in those trees there." He lighted a cigar, sheltering the lighter from both the wind and anyone who might be watching, and started the bike off slowly across the clearing and into the trees.

He sat straddling the bike, waiting for Reed and the other five men, hearing them approach a moment later at a run, Reed barking commands, "Bradley, get over there and keep a lookout. Michaelson, same for you but over there. Jackson, Cooley, Monro, take up positions along the tree line on that side about twenty or thirty yards apart. Move out! Alert is a long whistle, then two short." As the men started off, Reed called after them, "Everybody whistle?" Then he waved for them to go on, turned to Rourke, and fished out a cigarette. Rourke pulled out his lighter and flicked the wheel of the Zippo. Reed bent down to the flame cupped in Rourke's hands. "It's gettin' cold. You know, you miss that, no weather forecast, and then the weather has been changing so much."

"Yeah, I know," Rourke offered.

"So what are you doin' here?"

"Haven't seen a dark-haired woman and two children, maybe with another man and a woman and a child—little girl, I think—probably on horseback?"

"No," Reed said staring at the Harley. "Nothin' even close to that. Why?"

"My wife and children—saw some sign of them back about thirty miles, but it's from several weeks ago."

"But at least they're alive," Reed said, slapping

Rourke on the shoulder.

"Question is to find them though," Rourke said. Rourke opened up with few people he realized, and Reed—a nice enough guy, Rourke thought—wasn't one of them.

"Hey, listen," Reed said. "I could use a guy like you—ex-CIA, weapons specialist—you're from around here—could even give me the lay of the land."

"I'm otherwise occupied," Rourke said flatly.

"Yeah, but it's important."

"So's finding my wife and children, Reed," Rourke responded.

"I know that, but this is for the good of all of us."

"I don't really give a damn about the good of all of us. Organized government screwed things up the first time, it'll screw things up again. I'm finding my wife and children, and then I'll figure what kind of game I'm playing." Rourke started to ease up on his bike. Reed reached out and put his hand on Rourke's left arm. Rourke glared at him in the gathering shadow. "Don't!"

"Wait—maybe I can help you if you help me."

"I'm listening," Rourke told him.

"All right. Let me explain what we're doing."

"I don't care what you're doing, Reed. No offense, but I don't give a damn."

"Yeah, but I can help you find your woman and kids."

"How?" Rourke asked.

"We've got an intelligence network getting together, all sorts of places, use couriers, low-frequency radio—lots of ways of keeping in touch. If I put out the word that's dozens more pairs of eyes looking for them. How fast is one man going to find them? Huh?''

"What do you want?'' Rourke almost whispered.

"Some cooperation—maybe an extra hand with a gun if it comes to that. You in?''

"Just how good,'' Rourke rasped, "is that organization of yours, Reed, good enough, big enough to find Sarah?''

"We won't know unless we try. This'll maybe cost you a few days, maybe save you weeks or months, maybe make the difference for you in finding them or not.''

"I'll find them,'' Rourke stated. "Tell me what you're here for.''

"All right,'' Reed said, stomping out his cigarette butt on the ground.

"That's got a filter,'' Rourke said. "They take years to disintegrate; some kinds can take decades. Dead giveaway someone's been here, too.''

Reed looked at Rourke, then bent over, and picked up the cigarette butt, stripped away the paper and tobacco and pocketed the filter in the breast pocket of his camouflaged fatigue blouse. "Satisfied?'' Reed snapped.

Rourke nodded.

"Okay, then,'' Reed began again. "We're here for two reasons; We want a low down on the Soviet posture in Georgia—Karamatsov just got transferred in here on assignment—you should be interested in that.''

"Natalia,'' Rourke murmured.

"What?"

"Nothing," Rourke said, trying to mean it.

"All right, but the main reason we're here, and probably Karamatsov too, is we're looking for a guy—you might even know him—he has a place somewhere around here, vacation home. Name is Jim Colfax. He's an ex-astronaut, big shot in NASA public relations before the war."

"Why would anyone want him?"

"Ever hear of something called the Eden Project when you were with the company?"

Rourke thought for a moment. There were so many coded files, so many top-secret projects. But the Eden Project wasn't one he recalled.

"I haven't heard of it," Rourke told Reed.

"Well, neither had anybody else. We were sifting through the ruins of the Houston space center— found a charred file folder, and inside all we could make out was Eden Project, but nobody's left from NASA that we can find, except Colfax if he's still alive that is—and he should be right here in Georgia."

"Why, just because he had a vacation home here?"

"And he was speaking at the University in Athens the night before the bombing. It was the last engagement on a speaking tour, then he had a few weeks off."

"Hell of a way to spend a vacation—with a nuclear war," Rourke observed.

"Yeah, tell me about it," Reed said.

"So you want to find him to find out what the Eden Project was."

"We think it has to do with some launches at Cape Canaveral, just before the place got a direct hit—and we think the Russians are interested in it too."

Rourke looked up at the darkening sky. Was there someone up there, he wondered, or something that was a new horror. "I'll give you a description of my wife, my son, my daughter, the horses they were probably riding—then some poop on the Jenkins couple they might have been with—get it out as fast as you can. Got a radio?"

"Yeah, if I only use it a few minutes at a time so they can't peg us."

"You want my help," Rourke said, "then you get the description out—now. I'll write the details for you, and I'll listen while you send." Rourke fished a zippered notebook from his backpack on the back of the Harley, then began to write. He stopped. Was beautiful a valid description for Sarah, and how about Michael and Annie—handsome for him, cute for her? He decided on something more exact in nature.

An hour later, the message was sent and Rourke had committed to meet Reed and the others outside Athens at noon the following day. Two hours from the retreat, Rourke rode hard through the night.

Chapter 19

Rourke sat on the sofa, his hair still wet from the shower, a glass of whiskey in his right hand, a cigar burning in the ashtray beside him. Rubenstein had already eaten by the time Rourke returned, and nearly jumped out his skin, as Rourke had thought, when he'd seen Rourke walk in—three days early and with news of an American Intelligence team insertion in the area.

"Did Captain Reed ask about me?"

"No, sorry," Rourke told the younger man.

Rourke had fixed himself a can of stew and poured the beef, vegetables, and gravy over bread, then eaten it quickly. He sat in the great room, wanting to think. Finally, sipping at the top of his second drink, he shouted to Rubenstein, who was sitting on the far side of the room, reading. "Paul! What do you think— the Eden Project, something to do with Cape Canaveral—what does it suggest?"

Rubenstein seemed lost in thought for several moments, then looked up, and said, "Well, the Eden reference seems to mean some sort of beginning— maybe beginning again."

"Yeah," Rourke said.

"So, maybe it's some sort of manned flight that would have been too risky, unless there wasn't anything to lose—a lot of people thought the world would just get flattened after a full nuclear exchange—maybe it was some sort of space colonization effort or something."

"Or maybe just the opposite—a doomsday device. You've got to remember one thing, Paul, intelligence-operations names rarely have anything to do with the actual operation—just the opposite—so maybe a new beginning simply means a surprise ending."

"You mean some kind of superbomb orbiting the earth and timed to blow up soon?"

"Maybe not soon," Rourke said soberly. "Maybe not for five years, or ten years, or maybe the next five minutes. And maybe it's nothing we've thought of. I'll tell you what Reed wants me to do," Rourke said then, recounting his conversation with the Army captain and their scheduled meeting the next day. Rourke looked at his watch. It was already the next day—fifteen minutes into it.

The two men talked for a while longer. Afterward Rourke went to bed before Rubenstein. More to keep out the light than for privacy, Rourke drew the curtains separating the master bedroom from the rest of the cavern and stripped away his clothes, then lay down on the double bed, his left hand reaching out to the empty side of the bed, his mind filled with thoughts of Sarah.

Chapter 20

Rourke, Reed and three of the five Army men walked past the university, turned left, and walked to the downtown area of the city. Rourke's skin crawled. He was weaponless, not by choice, but necessity. To be caught with firearms or even a knife in the Soviet-occupied city would certainly mean discovery and most likely death. Rourke had decided on the course of action as the only means of contacting the Resistance. There was a man he knew in Athens and, if there were a Resistance forming, this man would be in it—Darren Ball, ex-Special Forces, ex-mercenary—tough, hard, experienced, and as anti-Communist as any man Rourke had ever met. Ball, before the war, had taken to running a bookstore specializing in militaria, weapons books, and related items. He had lost a leg in Rhodesia, which had effectively ended his military career.

Rourke, wearing a beat-up straw cowboy hat and

dark sunglasses, scanned the street. The sight of the Kalashnikov-armed Soviet troops strolling casually in the cold sunlight through an American city disgusted him. Twice Reed had had to restrain one of his men, Bradley, a young black sergeant, who was fiercely anti-Soviet.

With Reed and the three soldiers, all disguised as civilians and, like Rourke, weaponless, Rourke stopped on the corner. Without moving his lips, Rourke muttered, "Hope nobody stops us for papers or anything, hmm? Bradley, you come with Reed and me. You two drift around and act cool. We'll meet you back here. Try and assess the composition of the Russian units here; how many, what equipment—listen and learn—go," and without waiting for acquiescence, Rourke, Reed, and the headstrong Sgt. Bradley started toward where Rourke hoped to find Darren Ball, the Liberty Book Store and B.S. Emporium.

Almost brushing shoulders with a half-dozen Russian soldiers, Rourke, Reed, and Bradley reached the far corner, and Rourke stopped. The bookstore windows were boarded over and the wooden sign hanging over the storefront had been spray-painted black, lining out the name.

"What do we do now?" Reed asked.

"We keep our shirts on," Rourke said almost disgustedly, then slowly walked around the corner. A knot of young people was standing there, Rourke guessed in violation of some Russian rule against public assembly. Settling the straw cowboy hat low over his eyes, squinting in the sunlight despite the glasses he wore, Rourke walked over toward them, the two military men behind him. Rourke fished a small cigar out of the pocket of his snap-front cowboy shirt, and stopped beside the young men and women, bending his head low toward the flame of the Zippo held cupped in his hands, talking without looking at them, "Any of you people know what happened to the guy who used to run this place—the B.S. Emporium? Fella named Darren Ball, missing a leg."

One of the younger men looked squarely at Rourke, saying, "What—you want information? Go to hell."

A girl, about eighteen, grabbed the young man's arm as Rourke looked at him, the girl saying, "Cliff, don't. If he's one of them he'll only—"

"Relax," Rourke rasped, turning away and looking back into the street. "I'm an old friend of Darren Ball's. What are you so afraid of—if I'm one of who?"

He looked past the young man to the girl. She brushed her hair nervously from her face with the back of her left hand, her eyes shifting uneasily from side to side—they were pansy blue. "I didn't mean anything, Mister. Neither did he."

"I can take care of myself, Patty," the young man snapped, stepped toward Rourke, shaking the girl's restraining hand from his arm.

Rourke turned, faced the young man, glanced from side to side on the street, and smashed his right knee up, higher than for a groin shot, just smacking into the stomach in the soft part of the gut, and as the young man—Cliff, Rourke remembered the girl calling him—doubled over, Rourke flicked his right hand down across the left side of the boy's neck, the knife edge chopping above the musculature and behind the ear. The young man collapsed. Rourke caught him under the armpits and got the boy—unconscious—to his feet.

"Here, you and you," Rourke snapped swaying the unconscious Cliff toward two of the other young men in the crowd. They had been edging toward Rourke, but catching Cliff had forced them to move back.

Rourke drew his lips back over his teeth, inhaling hard on his cigar, then exhaling the gray smoke, watching it catch the wind as he scanned the street on both sides for evidence that he had been watched. It seemed clear. He looked at the girl. "Patty, now tell me what you mean—you think I'm spying for the Russians. What?"

"I—I didn't say that," the girl stammered.

Rourke bent toward her, his face inches from hers, her eyes looking up into his. He removed the glasses, saying, "I'm not going to tell you why I want to see Darren Ball. That would only maybe get you in trouble. He and I are old friends and if you dislike the Russians as much as you seem to fear them, then you should tell me—now. Do you know where he is?"

"I'm afraid," she said, looking nervously from side to side. "You don't have to do anything wrong. The Russians pay for informers and people have started informing on anyone whether he's done something or not, and sometimes they let you go after it—sometimes they kill you. My sister—they let her go. She hadn't done anything, but she hasn't

114

opened her mouth to say a single word since—" She drew in her breath hard and it made a sort of scream, Rourke thought. He glanced behind him: six Russians, armed, were rounding the corner.

Rourke looked at her. "Now—quick—where?"

"A tent down by the fire station—all I—"

"You—the cowboy hat!" The voice was hard, young, filled with authority. Over the years Rourke had come not only to distrust authority but to resent it.

Rourke turned around. Reed and Bradley had drifted off, and he could see them across the street. "Yeah?"

"You're supposed to say—" the girl started behind him.

"That is an improper form of address," the young Russian lieutenant snapped.

"Well, what am I supposed to call you?"

Rourke knew the drill, he thought, and under normal circumstances, he realized, he would have played the game to get away quietly and do his business, but the fear in the girl's eyes made him think differently. The Russian and his five men edged toward Rourke. Rourke put his sunglasses back on, rolled the cigar in his mouth to the left corner, the half-burnt cigar clamped in his teeth there.

"I asked you a question. What am I supposed to call you? How about wimp? That seems to fit you real good, boy."

"What is this wimp?" the young Russian officer asked.

Rourke heard laughter from behind him. Rourke looked down at the toes of his cowboy boots—they went with the hat—and then up into the young Soviet officer's eyes. "Gee, that's hard to explain, boy, sort of like a pussy-whip. Ever hear of that?"

"Pussy what?"

"Here," Rourke began. "I'll show you." And Rourke started to reach into his breast pocket as if for the stub of pencil sticking out there, then swung his right arm back in a broad arc, the knife edge of his hand smashing hard against the young Russian's windpipe, smashing it, killing the boy. Rourke's left hand flashed down to the brown leather flap holster on the officer's belt, and grabbed at the pistol there as he shoved the already dead Russian back against his five men, Rourke's left hand on the automatic, his right hand snapping back the slide—a Makarov PM 9mm—just in case there hadn't been a chambered round, his left first finger pulling back on the trigger. The gun fired point blank in the face of a Russian sergeant standing immediately behind the dead officer.

Rourke started to run, into the street, across it. The other four Russians, shouting angrily, started into the street behind him. He caught Reed's eye, shook his head. "No!" He kept running, then turned, snapped off two shots, the Soviet pistol in his right hand now. One more of the Russians went down.

He could see Bradley, the black American intelligence sergeant, starting into the street, bent down beside the dead Russian, then his hands came up, an AK-47 at his hip, the gun spitting fire. Rourke ducked behind a painted-over mailbox, fired two more rounds. A Soviet soldier fell less than six feet from him. Rourke lunged toward the dead man into the street, away from the mailbox, rolled as the pavement around him chewed up in fragments of tar and concrete, his hands on the AK-47 the Russian soldier had dropped, the pistol clattering to the pavement, his fingers searching out the safety on the Kalashnikov as he rolled. Suddenly there were more than a dozen Soviet soldiers in the street, guns firing everywhere around him. He stopped in mid-roll, got to one knee, fired, his first three-round burst catching the last of the original six Russians.

On his feet, Rourke ran toward the far sidewalk, Bradley beside him, his AK-47 firing. Rourke grabbed at the man, swinging him around roughly by his shoulder, shouting, "Hothead!" Then he ran down the sidewalk, better than a dozen Russian soldiers after them, the crowd of unemployed, listless citizens parting like waves before them—men and women with the life drained from their eyes ducking into abandoned storefronts to escape the Soviet gunfire and the two men, Rourke thought, the two madmen fighting the Russians.

Rourke glanced behind him, saw the pansy-eyed girl fleeing unmolested. Rourke had killed the men who could have caused her trouble. Then he saw Reed running after her. Rourke, firing a burst from the AK-47, ducked into a gangway between two buildings, Bradley beside him.

At the end of the gangway there was a concrete fence blocking his way. Rourke stopped, glanced behind him once, then at the nearest wall. He thought bitterly that if it had been a movie scenario there would have been a fire escape, but it wasn't a movie. Instead there were staggered rows of wooden-framed windows in the concrete, the sills large enough, Rourke hoped. He reached up, the AK-47 slung across his back diagonally, his right foot purchased against the sill of the lowest window, then pushed himself up, bracing his foot against the center of the window where it opened, pushing himself, clawing the concrete to grasp the lowest portion of the next higher sill, his legs swinging free a moment, his hands tearing away from the rough and splintering wood under the weight of his body, then his right leg swinging up for a purchase, finding it, Rourke pulled himself upward, snatching at the center of the window frame.

Rourke glanced below him—gunfire. Bradley was spraying the far end of the gangway, the dozen or so Soviet soldiers temporarily stopped there. Rourke started up again, hearing the gunfire below him stop. He glanced down; Bradley was ripping the banana-shaped magazine from the AK-47, throwing it to the gangway surface. Rourke started to reach back to his own gun, to strip the magazine from it, then thought better of it.

Looking up, Rourke could see the roof line. He pushed himself up, both feet angled against the windowsill, his hands flat against the building sides, then he reached up, pushing up from the center of the window, his right hand grasping for the roof-line edge, his mouth open, shouting, "Bradley! Come on, man—after me!"

His fingertips could barely touch the roof line. Rourke looked down. The Russian troops were starting into the gangway, firing, Bradley pulling back.

Rourke pushed himself up, jumping for the roof edge, his fingers over the edge, slipping, his nails digging into the rotted wood and rusty metal, his hands holding, his right foot braced against the top of the highest window, his left leg swinging free in the air.

Getting his left foot against the window, he half jumped, half shoved himself upward, his right hand over the edge of the roof line, then his left, then his right leg swinging up.

Rourke flattened against the roof line—no time for a breath—wheeling to his knees, the muzzle of the AK-47 over the roofline, Rourke fired it into the Russians advancing through the gangway, the soldiers drawing back and firing back at him.

He looked over the side, shouting down to Bradley, "Come on, man!"

And Bradley, the useless and empty AK on the gangway surface, started for the first window. Rourke fired another three-round burst, covering the black sergeant. Bradley was reaching for the second window, then, shorter than Rourke, barely got his hands to the higher ledge and pulled himself up. Rourke fired another burst at the end of the gangway. Bradley was on the second window ledge, half up, reaching for the roof line, his fingers splayed against the wall, but a good six inches too short to touch it.

Rourke dropped the AK, pulling his belt from the loops of his jeans, snaking it over the roof line. Bradley reached for it and grabbed it. The belt in Rourke's right hand, he fired another three-round burst with the AK from his left.

Bradley's right hand was on the roof line, then

Rourke felt the tension on the belt slacken as Bradley's left hand reached up, Rourke snatching for it with his right, his fist locking around the black man's wrist. Rourke fired the AK-47—it was empty.

Bradley clambered over the edge of the roof line. Rourke stood, hurtling the AK over the side on a Russian soldier trying to scale the wall.

"Come on!" Rourke rasped, starting across the roof. At the far side he saw a fire escape, started toward it as a Russian soldier came on to the roof, his AK-47 coming on line.

The belt was still in Rourke's right hand, and he swung it, the heavy trophy buckle lashing across the Soviet soldier's right cheek and nose, opening a gash in the face. The man fell back toward the edge of the roof. Rourke dove for him, catching him, snatching the AK-47 still clutched in the man's hands, then snatched the utility belt and the spare magazines there.

"Here!" he shouted to Bradley, throwing him the gun and the belt, then Rourke shoved the half conscious Russian over the edge of the roof. The man's body hurtled down on the Russians streaming up the fire escape below him.

Rourke scanned the roof line. There was another building beyond, the roof at approximately the same height.

"Come on!" he rasped to the sergeant. "Just like television—" Rourke started in a deadrun for the far edge of the roof, jumped, his legs extended in midair between the building, his body crashing down on the neighboring roof, going into a roll.

Bradley had stopped on the edge. "Catch the

gun." He tossed the AK-47 across the airspace, then the belt. Rourke looped the belt across his shoulders and under his right arm. Bradley ran back, then started forward, bent against his stride and his face set, his lips drawn back.

"Look out!" Rourke shouted. Bradley cleared the roof line as a Soviet soldier came up by the fire escape, his AK-47 opening up.

Bradley's arms flew away from his sides, like a bird trying to fly, a look of fear on his face for a fleeting instant, then the eyes wide. Bradley was dead; his body fell between the buildings. Rourke dropped to both knees and opened up with the AK-47, a three-round burst hammering into the face of the Russian who'd killed the black sergeant.

Rourke got to his feet, backing away, knowing the Russians were coming up the fire escape. He scanned the roof he was on: there were no buildings near, no hope of escape, he thought. The AK-47 braced against his right hip in an assault position, Rourke started to squeeze the trigger of the AK, then spun to his right. From the far end of the downtown section there was an explosion, then a fireball belched up into the sky.

"The fire station!" Rourke rasped. "Reed—Darren Ball!" Rourke edged toward the far side of the roof, the street below him in panic, fire belching up from manhole covers and sewers.

Rourke turned. Three Russian soldiers were coming up on the opposite roof. He fired, burning out the magazine, then rammed home a fresh one from the belt.

A truck was parked by the curb on the street side,

a pickup with a camper top over it. "What the hell!" Rourke rasped. He took a few steps back from the roof edge to get up momentum, then with a running jump clear of the roof, crashed down toward the camper top, his body impacting hard against it, sliding off, and rolling down into the street.

Rourke pulled himself to his feet. There was a single Russian starting toward the roof line above. Rourke raised the muzzle of the AK-47 and fired a three-round burst, then turned and ran, as the Soviet soldier fell screaming from the roof onto the street. The fires still raged from the manhole covers. Sirens were wailing in the distance.

Chapter 21

Varakov's one abiding wish ever since assuming military command of the Army of Occupation had been, he thought, a simple and basic one—he would have preferred that Lake Michigan be facing west of the city so he could watch the sunset over it. He walked along the lakeshore, watching the deep blue of the water, then looking beyond toward the city he commanded and wondering about the country that lay beyond it. He walked along stone ramparts, slick and slippery from the water, but he walked very carefully, watching the waves break below him. Finally, he sat, staring out at the darkening water, thinking.

Karamatsov had to die—yes. But Karamatsov was the favored child of the KGB, and simply to walk up to him and shoot him in the face would not go well. To try to implicate him in some impropriety would perhaps bring about the downfall of Natalia as well.

And, Varakov realized, if he attempted to arrange for something concerning Karamatsov and it were to fail, then matters would only be worse: it could come back at him and only diminish his power and his ability to protect Natalia from Karamatsov and from her own warped sense of guilt.

No, it had to be a death, pure and simple. And if he could arrange the death in such a way as to make Karamatsov appear the hero, the valiant, noble—but thoroughly dead—Soviet officer, that would only serve to heighten Natalia's security—and his own. He worried enough about the latter only to be realistic. He realized he was an old man and from Soviet political standards, he was almost as old as one could justifiably expect to become.

A hero's death for Karamatsov. The man in charge of the American Continental KGB would die a hero. Yes.

But as to how he could assure Karamatsov's memory, Varakov felt at a loss. He needed, he realized, to somehow make certain someone from the Americans would kill Karamatsov. And, Varakov sighed, Karamatsov was very good, hard to kill—deadly and skillful and well protected.

To kill Karamatsov he would need someone who could best him, someone who was even more deadly, more skillful. A smile flashed across his thick lips. The man who had however unwittingly started it all, the fight between Karamatsov and Natalia—what was the name? Varakov stood up, staring out at the water. The wind was whipping up, some of the breakers now crashing over the lips of the nearest edge of concrete. "Rourke," he said, so only the water could hear him . . . .

"Comrade General?"

"Girl, coffee!" he shouted, walking, he realized, as he hadn't walked since he was ten years younger. He smiled at the young female secetary, and shouted after her as she scurried downstairs to the cafeteria for the coffee, "And requisition a new uniform skirt; that one is too long!"

He crashed down in the chair behind his desk, his greatcoat still on, plopping his hat on the desk top and kicking off his shoes.

"Rourke," he said, "who has bested Karamatsov once before. Ha, ha!"

Chapter 22

Rourke had hidden the Harley and his weapons in the railroad yard by the end of town. With the explosions still ringing in the distance, he edged toward the area cautiously through the tall grass and weeds, the reddish clay under his feet giving because of the dampness of the ground. He could see two of Reed's men left behind with the equipment. He edged closer to them and, in a low voice, called out. The men turned, guns ready, but the muzzles already lowering as Rourke rose from his crouch and ran across the few yards separating them.

"What the hell is goin' on in that town—Fourth of July or a war?"

"A little of both, I guess," Rourke answered, sitting in the grass despite the dampness, shucking off the cowboy boots and exchanging them for his black combat boots. "Bradley's dead—shot by some Soviet trooper—but I got the guy. Reed and the others are okay. He made contact with the

Resistance, I'm almost certain." Rourke scraped most of the mud off the cowboy boots, slipped them into a plastic bag, and secured them inside the Lowe pack on the back of the Harley, then scrounged out his weapons, checking the twin Detonics pistols, the Government .45, and the CAR-15. "We can wait a little while, but not too long—I don't want the Russians slamming up roadblocks and putting out more patrols and us getting boxed in." Rourke slipped on the brown leather jacket over his double Alessi holster, then left the bike, starting toward one of the crumbling concrete pylons supporting the railroad trestle. He noticed Reed's two men behind him.

"You," Rourke said to the nearest man, not remembering his name and not bothering to read the cloth tag sewn onto his cammie fatigues. "Go over there to my left, on the far side in the weeds and wait. Keep that intersection as your field of fire." He turned to the other man, pointed along the railroad tracks, and rasped, "You take up a position about fifty yards down there and spot the road. I'll keep an eye out here. And don't get overeager and shoot anything that moves; there're a lot of civilians out there, hmm?"

As both men left, Rourke crouched in the grass, the CAR-15 across his lap, the scope covers off and the stock extended. He could hear the wind despite the distant rumblings from the city, and as he watched beyond the tracks for some sign of Reed or the others, or for some sign of Russian troops, he reviewed what had happened. Once the young Russian officer had come up to him, it meant an arrest—and if nothing else a short period of detention.

But, more likely, Rourke thought, it meant his identification. He was certain that after he'd helped President Chambers break out from the KGB Texas stronghold, all KGB units had the Soviet equivalent of a rap sheet on him—a physical description at the least and, likely, a photo of him fished from old KGB files when he'd been on the CIA active list years before. And that young girl, Rourke thought, the one with the pansy eyes—there'd been a look of fear in her eyes, the same look he'd seen in the eyes of the people he and Bradley had run past when the Soviet troops had been pursuing them. The people in Athens, Rourke thought bitterly, probably the people in any occupied American city needed something to show them the Soviets weren't invincible. Rourke smiled. He knew they weren't.

Rourke dropped on the ground, the butt of the CAR-15 swinging up to his shoulder, the crosshairs of the three power scope settling on something moving on the far side of the triple crossroads beyond the tracks. It was hard to see clearly because the road curved deeply and was partially out of view.

He saw the movement again, wishing the Steyr-Mannlicher SSG were with him rather than at the retreat because of the doubleset triggers, the tolerances in the barrel and the action. You could make reliable hits with the SSG out to a thousand yards and sometimes beyond. A smile crossed his lips. The semi-automatic version of Colonel Colt's little assault rifle would have to do. As he watched across the eye relief into and through the scope, he thought about the gun for a moment—there were more expensive assault type sporters than the

CAR-15, but for his use, none he truly liked better—spare parts, spare magazines, ammunition, all were out there to be found, scrounged from a military rifle, whatever. And, despite his comparatively vast experience with weapons, Rourke abhorred guns that were complicated to clean or maintain.

He saw the movement again, this time clearly through the scope tube, then relaxed. It was Reed, and not far behind him—Rourke swept the scope along—were the two other men who had been with him. And behind them—Rourke settled the crosshairs on the awkwardly moving man—was a fourth figure. The figure turned; Rourke caught the face under the objective lens—Darren Ball, prosthetic leg and all.

Rourke leaned back in the tall grass and stared skyward. He wondered without verbalizing it if Darren Ball and men like himself as well had been more a cause for the problems that had brought the war—more a cause than a solution. Then he thought back to the girl with the pansy-colored eyes: there was no reason for fear, no reason why it should be endured or allowed to grow. Ball, in his own way as an anti-Communist mercenary, had fought that fear. Rourke had fought it in the CIA, since by working against the ignorance that helped fear that made men in situations where their lives and other lives were at stake do the wrong thing, or fear to do anything because it could be wrong.

Rourke shook his head, got back into a crouch, a smile crossing his lips, his hands almost without conscious will collapsing the stock on the CAR-15, replacing the elastic connected scope covers, flicking the CAR-15's safety to the on position. He edged along the grass toward the nearest of the concrete pylons and stood up to his full height, waiting.

It took a full three minutes by the face of the Rolex Submariner for Ball, Reed, and the others to reach the railroad trestle. Already Rourke was getting edgey over the protracted time. Rourke signaled the men as they approached, waving them over by the crumpling pylon, Ball's face creasing into a smile as he saw Rourke. The man limped forward, short of breath. "John! Hell man, I thought they'd gotten you!"

The two men shook hands, then Rourke said, "Darren, have you heard anything?"

"Reed already asked me," Ball said.

Rourke looked at Reed and nodded. Rourke added, "Well—have you?"

"All I know is somebody told me as they passed by your place the end of the first day after the war—saw a bunch of tire tracks and some hoof prints from maybe four or five horses—fella wasn't sure on that. The house was burned down, but it was still hot. Coupl'a bodies too, some burned up, some not—three, maybe four, people, one of them a woman. Found a couple of guns burned up in the house—they yours?"

"No. All I had at the house was a shotgun and a .45. Sarah probably took those—least I hope she did," Rourke added.

"She doesn't know where that fancy-dan retreat of yours is, huh?"

Rourke looked at Ball, saying, "She could have,

but we never got around to it. I'm the only one who knows," he said, intentionally neglecting to mention Paul Rubenstein. He didn't know how far he wanted to trust Ball, despite their long-standing semi-friendship.

"Well, I'll put the word out to look for her—and the kids. Now what do you want in Athens besides causing trouble?"

Rourke smiled, then his voice low, said, "Ask these guys—they've got the big ideas. I'm just the native guide."

Ball laughed, then turned to Reed. "You want that Jim Colfax—tonight's the best time to do your askin'—and you guys can give us a hand."

He looked at Rourke.

Rourke looked up from his watch. "Let's cut the small talk—time's wasting."

"I'll make it short then," Ball said, his whiskey voice almost hiding a laugh. "We got a raid planned tonight—a biggee. I can't go, but Rourke—if you go and bring some of these fellas along, well—I'll make certain the whole Resistance network has the poop on Sarah and the kids—and on Colfax." Ball, edging painfully it appeared on his false leg, glanced at Reed.

"Where?" Rourke said, cutting off Reed before the Army Intelligence man could speak.

"Nine o'clock or so at the old drive-in down the highway. You know the place?"

"Yeah," Rourke sighed. "Check your watch against mine."

Ball pulled from his jeans pocket a wristwatch with a broken band. Comparing their times, Rourke was about ten minutes fast.

"I'll go by your time," Rourke rasped.

"Hey, John?" Ball said as Rourke turned to move back toward the Harley.

Rourke looked at him, saying, "I forgot to say thanks for the fireworks—bailed me out, Darren."

"You cost us, John. Full dress tonight. There's gonna be a lot of killin'."

Rourke looked at Ball, watched the gray eyes, smiled, and just shook his head and started for the Harley. "A lot of killing," he muttered under his breath. He would have thought there'd been enough of that despite the fact that it was a likely consequence it would have at least ceased to be a preoccupation.

Killing. Some people never changed, Rourke thought.

Chapter 23

Natalia sat on the couch. Her face was still tender where it was bruised. She moved her body slowly to get a more comfortable position; the welts on her back made it awkward to sit. She rearranged the long robe around her as she tucked her legs up onto the sofa, and hugged her knees to her. Karamatsov, she thought, Vladmir.

She sipped at the vodka, feeling the ice against her even white teeth. Would her uncle try to get revenge against Vladmir? The thought chilled her more than the ice. She brushed a strand of black hair away off her forehead and wrapped the blue terrycloth robe around her more tightly. She glanced at the digital clock on the table beside the sofa. Her uncle, General Ishmael Varakov, had called twenty-five minutes before to tell her he was coming to see her. Why?

There was a knock at the door, the one repaired

133

only a few hours earlier. It was the sound of a fist, rather than the metallic *click-click-click* of the brass doorknocker.

She stood up, tightened the belt around the robe, and reached into the small drawer of the end table. She had put away the gun she'd taken from Vladmir and had the little four-barreled stainless steel COP pistol. She broke the pistol, verified all four barrels were loaded, and dropped the double action only derringer-like gun in the right pocket of her robe. Her hand remained there. It was likely her uncle, she thought, but chances were something only fools took. She stopped, the thought momentarily amusing her. Hadn't it been a chance to marry the most handsome and most ruthless young officer in the KGB? Some chances didn't prove out, she thought, staring at the unopened door at the end of the small hallway, hearing the knocking again.

She walked to the door, decided against peering through the peephole, and stood beside the doorframe in the narrow part by the wall. She asked through the door, in Russian, "Yes, who is at the door?"

"It is cold out here, and I'm an old man too lazy to button his coat. Hurry, girl!"

She smiled. Natalia loved her uncle like a second father, perhaps more than the father she had lost as a little girl. She verified it was him by glancing through the magnifying lens in the peephole, then released the chain and the deadbolt, and swung the door inward.

The old man stood there, his greatcoat open as he'd told her, rubbing his gloved hands together. He took a step inside, and she let him smother her in his arms as he had always done since she was a child.

"Uncle," she murmured.

"Child," he whispered, then, one arm still around her, he started into the hall. "It is cold here—like Moscow—only somehow more damp." With his free hand he swung the door shut behind them.

They stopped at the end of the hall beside the steps leading down into the living room. She helped him out of his coat, took his hat and gloves, and watched him as he walked into the living room. Hugging the coat to her, she walked back into the hall and hung it on the coat tree and set the hat on the small table, then, taking a deep breath because she was afraid of what her uncle would say, she walked back toward the living room, and down the steps. Natalia sat beside him on the couch, tucking her knees up and her ankles under her again, looking at his deep, almost canine-sad, eyes.

"Natalia, I need information and I will not tell you why. You doubtless already suspect why at any event, child. You may keep your suspicions. I want information."

"Uncle?"

"Fix me vodka, then I will tell you." He picked up her glass, sniffed at it and smiled, then looked at the ice, his face downturning at the corners of the mouth. "None of this American ice-cube mixing—a ruination of good vodka."

She smiled and leaned across the couch, still on her knees, and kissed his cheek, then got up, walked into the kitchen.

She could hear him humming. *Hey! Andrushka,*

the song itself about drinking vodka. She poured a tumbler about two-thirds full and brought the bottle out with it, and returned to the living room.

He abruptly stopped humming as she re-entered the room. She handed him the glass, and he drank it down neat, exhaled hard and rasped, his voice odd-sounding and breathless.

"It is not like the vodka we made when I was a boy—you used pepper or sand or whatever you could get to make the oil float to the bottom, so it would not go into your mouth with the vodka—ughh. Lovely thing it was!"

She laughed, and poured him another glass. He looked at it for a while, not drinking it. She sat beside him and took her own glass. The ice was near-ly melted.

"What do you want to know, Uncle?"

"I want to know the name of the man Vladmir had in Samuel Chambers's inner circle—the traitor to the new President. I want the man's name, his title or official duties, and how he may be contacted. I want this all now." And Varakov tossed down the vodka.

Natalia watched his hands. She wondered what they were truly capable of.

Chapter 24

Sarah Rourke sat on the steps of the front porch, listening to the kitchen sounds Mary made, watching the reddish orb of sun in the low, thin clouds at the end of what was a peaceful universe for her—or perhaps, she thought, an island, an island of normalcy in the fear and hatred and terror of the world since the war.

She stood up, her feet in borrowed shoes, smoothed the borrowed dress against her as she walked into the house through the screen door and through the perfectly normal living room or parlor, past the long dining-room table, already set, and through the narrow hall past the pantry into the kitchen. She liked older houses, despite the sometimes awkward room arrangements.

Mary—Millie's aunt—was standing by the kitchen sink, rinsing vegetables.

"Can I help with dinner, Mary?" Sarah asked.

"No need, Sarah, but you can if you like. I need those potatoes peeled, knife over in the top drawer, and there's an apron on the hook other side of the door."

"Okay," Sarah said, finding the apron and tying it around her waist. She found the knife and sat at the small table and opened the cloth sack of potatoes. "What do I put the peelings in?"

Mary turned around from the sink, the water still running. She didn't say anything for a minute, then, "I'd say open a newspaper. We used to open an old newspaper. But there ain't none. We used to use a grocery sack. Old Mr. Harland ran the grocery, but he died of a heart attack when they busted into the grocery—drove their trucks and motorcycles right through the glass windows they did—killed some of the clerks who were trying to help old Mr. Harland." Mary rubbed her hands on the front of her apron, turned around absently, and shut off the water.

Sarah watched the woman, watched as Mary stared through the window above the sink and into the garden and beyond. Sarah could see the purplish night far off in the distance. She heard a sniffing sound, saw Mary bend down and touch the apron to her face, then heard the water turn back on. Mary was talking, but not looking at Sarah.

"I don't know, Sarah—where to put them peels from them potatoes. I don't know."

Chapter 25

Rourke watched in the shadows. It was a commando raid, he guessed, something against a Soviet installation in the city or somewhere near. He had left the bike for two of Reed's men to guard as well as Reed's other equipment.

Then with Reed and the other two surviving team members, Rourke had started walking through the woods and paralleled the road for about a mile, seeing no sign of traffic as they made their way toward the old drive-in theater. Rourke knew the man and woman who'd owned it years before, and now as he turned off the road and skirted behind it, avoiding the access drive, he wondered if somehow the couple had managed to make it through the holocaust.

He felt someone tapping on his shoulder and heard a whisper—Reed's voice. "Why are we taking the long way around, Rourke?"

Rourke stopped, the CAR-15 slung from his right

shoulder, his fist wrapped on the pistol grip, the safety lever on and his thumb near it. "I trust the motives of the Resistance people, but there could always be a ringer in with them, working for the Soviets."

"Goddamn Russians," Reed muttered.

Rourke looked at him, able to discern the outline of his face in the darkness, saying, his voice low, "Yeah, well, maybe goddamn Communists, but not goddamn Russians—they're people just like we are, led by their government—doing what they're told."

"You were sweet on that Russian broad a little, weren't you? Chambers said she—"

Rourke jabbed the muzzle of the CAR-15 forward, hard in the darkness, a moan and a rush of air issuing from Reed's lips as he doubled over. Bending beside him, the muzzle of the rifle alongside the hunched-over man's face, Rourke rasped, "You keep out of my personal affairs, Reed, hear that? And not that it's any of your business, because it damned well isn't, if it weren't for that 'Russian broad' your President would have been locked away by the Communist occupation forces by now and you and all your people would have been croaked in a neutron blast. It doesn't matter how I feel about her, she did us all a good turn and got her own tail in a sling probably doin' it. And I wouldn't be here doin' this foolishness to begin with if I weren't trying to find my wife and kids. You grow up a little, and maybe you're gonna realize that any normal man meets a lot of 'broads' like you call 'em, a lot of women he can like, maybe he could love under different circumstances. But it's only juvenile delinquents and morons who figure fidelity's a one-way street. I figure if my wife counts me as alive, wherever she is, she's being faithful to me—and I don't just owe her the same, I want to give her the same. Now—" and Rourke bent low, his lips almost touching Reed's ear, his voice rasping and hard—"you think you got all that, Reed? Or you wanna go out back there a few hundred yards into the brush and get the shit kicked out of you?"

Even in the dark, Rourke could see the hard set around Reed's eyes. "You give sermons, too, huh? Mr. Good Guy, Mr. Hero, what's some dinky-assed nuclear war to you, huh?"

Rourke let out a slow, low breath, saying half through his teeth, "You and the guys like you who stayed with the system are the ones who fucked it all up. Had to play your little games, do your little dances, keep the world spinning around and figure when it stopped it was like a roulette wheel—you win, fine, you lose, there's always another game. Well, you look at the sunsets, you feel the temperatures against your skin, you measure the rainfall, you count the dead bodies, sucker. Some Communist gave an attack order, some guy over here gave an attack order and it's just real great to push some goddamn anonymous button. You go out and kill a couple hundred million people some night when you can smell their sweat, smell it when they die and their bowels loosen up and their sphincters relax, and you can see the eyes go glassy. You do it that way next time, and see how well you like playin'."

Rourke turned around and started through the

brush toward the main parking area of the abandoned drive-in, somehow feeling better inside and at
the same time feeling worse. He'd always labeled
himself either laid back or uptight—he'd never been
sure which. And he wasn't used to hearing himself
let go. His jaw set, he kept walking.

Rourke edged toward the farthest end of the tall
standing pine trees, their bare shadows casting long,
thin lines along the ground from the reflected light
of Coleman lanterns in the center of the drive-in lot.
Rourke watched the assembled men—no women. He
didn't like the rendezvous; it was too open. He
waited as the now-silent Reed edged up near him.

The man rasped, "After this is through, you and
me."

Rourke simply nodded. Reed, competent, tough
and—Rourke thought—about as bull-headed as he,
was the last thing on his mind.

Chapter 26

General Varakov sat in darkness. Other than the
light from the long rectangular lamp that bathed his
desk in yellow, beyond was shadow and then beyond
it blackness, and far into the main hall near the
skeletons of the mastodons was a ceiling light, but it
shone more like a beacon than a source of illumination. The light cast shadows from the bones of the
two prehistoric giants and seemed only to accentuate
how they somehow did not fit in the real world of
men and yet emphasized the mortality they shared
with men.

Varakov wiped his hands across his eyes, and
stared at the file folder. It was the KGB file on John
Thomas Rourke. He scanned through it once again.
Doctor of Medicine, with no particular specialty,
and training toward general practice, and after the
degree, internship at—Varakov didn't recognize the
name of the hospital. After there was an unac-

counted-for year, and then Rourke had joined Central Intelligence as a case officer—the translation for that Varakov knew was a spy, an agent. He had moved into the Black Section—Covert Operations, and had killed several times for the agency, targets usually in Latin America. Varakov noted with interest that apparently Karamatsov and Rourke had crossed paths in Latin America once. And Rourke had bested Karamatsov.

For some reason not clear in the file, Rourke had quit Central Intelligence after an affair in Latin America, which he'd barely survived. There had been an ambush, Rourke's people had been killed, and only Rourke's body had not been found, and then several weeks later a man matching Rourke's general description had been seen near the docks and after that, Rourke had apparently drifted into Miami, barely alive.

His nerve gone? Varakov doubted that, for after leaving CIA Rourke had begun to freelance, not in Intelligence, but in counter-terrorist training, survival training, weapons skills, etc. He had been spotted working with pro-American military and police units in virtually every corner of the world where the Americans needed the help most. Varakov made a mental note to see if Rourke had really left the Company, as it was called, or simply assumed a cover.

Rourke had written several books on the medical, psychological, and weapons-related aspects of survival—short and long-term. He was an expert; Varakov noted curiously that some of Rourke's works had been pirated, translated, and were adapted as training manuals in the Soviet Union. The thought amused him; he wondered if Rourke would take such knowledge well? He doubted it. He scanned through the family background; wife works as an artist, illustrator, and writer of children's books; two children, Michael and Ann. Varakov worked the dates—the boy would be nearing seven, the girl nearing five.

He scanned through the file to the skills section. There was a repeat of the medical background, the standard things one expected in an Intelligence agent, or former agent, dealing with radio, etc. He was qualified on helicopters, fixed-wing aircraft, military jets. Rourke's Georgia driver's license number appeared there—curiously, Varakov thought—the same as Rourke's social security number. He was reportedly an expert marksman, but that was to be expected. Habitually carried .45ACP or .357 Magnum-caliber handguns.

Perfect—he'd liked the sound of the man when he'd spoken with him and realized that despite their political, ideological, and other differences, to Varakov's thinking, they were much alike. Men of purpose, men with feeling, men who did what they must. Varakov had never liked Karamatsov who had no feeling, and when the surface was finally scratched, the insides were worse than those of a pig.

Natalia was his special child, Varakov scowled—and for hurting her, Karamatsov would simply and finally die. Varakov did not consider it revenge, and the justice of it was not something that bothered him either. It was just—but more to the point—it was something he wanted done. He sighed, not being a vindictive man, but wishing that circumstance did not preclude him pulling the trigger himself.

His desk phone rang.

"Varakov!" he snapped into the receiver. It was the radio room, his contact.

He waited, thinking about how to handle the man, waiting while the adjustments were made. This was the traitor in President Chambers's closest group of advisors.

"Hello, yes, Varakov. So—at last. You, too, are a general of sorts I hear," Varakov said, the thought slightly amusing him. He disliked traitors, and the more highly placed, however useful, the more intense the dislike.

"Yes, sir," the very American, cowboyish voice answered noncommittally.

"Randan Soames, Commander of the Paramilitary forces of Texas, one of Samuel Chambers's trusted confidants. A man who visited Russia twelve years ago, has been working for us ever since and has, before the war, handed us over numerous copies of secret files coming through your electronics components businesses. How nice to meet you," Varakov said.

"Yes, sir."

"I understand that you sexually molested a child—"

"Sir, please, I beg—"

"I, personally, would not have chosen blackmailing you into espionage. I would have shot you. You are worse than a savage, worse than an animal. I would have no compunction against leaking to your

American friends who you are, what you have done for us and why. That is clear?'' Varakov wanted to terminate the conversation as quickly as possible, feeling somehow dirty talking with the man even across perhaps several thousand miles. He wasn't quite certain exactly how far Texas was from Chicago.

"But, General Varakov—"

"You will do exactly as I say—I am a man of honor and you are not—therefore, you are taking advantage of me and you have nothing to lose. I need the following. I understand this American terrorist Rourke is obsessed with locating his wife and children who were living in Georgia before the war. All indications would be that he has gone there. How can he be found—immediately?''

"But, sir, I, ahh—"

"You will find him for me, tell me how he can be located precisely, and all will be as it was. If you do not, then all will be bad for you. I will hear from you in two hours. You would have more time had you contacted me sooner as requested.''

"But, sir, I had to be so careful so no one—"

"I am not interested in these concerns, however genuine. Do your job—now!'' Varakov hung up the receiver and checked his watch. He shut off the desk lamp and sat in the dark better to study the shadows of the bones from the central hall. He answered the telephone, not bothering with the light, and because of the darkness somehow he found himself speaking more softly that he had the first time.

"Yes, Soames. A team lead by a Captain Reed—you will be left alone—that is my pledge.

147

Yes, Reed has reported his position. Near where? Ahh," Varakov remembered the name of the town where he had set up the garrison. "A raid of some kind. That should be easy to determine. You learn, as a real—" and he emphasized the last word— "military commander that there are certain things no Resistance fighter or terrorist bothers with—you may want to keep them busy with these by making them attractive—a bank with no money, a warehouse filled with empty boxes, like this. And, conversely, there are certain targets no self-respecting Resistance fighter will pass up. That is why they die so quickly. You have done satisfactorily. You are safe." And then, his voice low, he added, "But, if it ever comes to me that you touch another child, I will come after you and kill you myself with my bare hands." He smashed the receiver down.

He lifted the receiver again, pushed the button, and got the staff office downstairs. "This is Varakov. Contact immediately the Commander of the Southeast Regional District and get him on my line—have my personal plane fueled and ready, and find my secretary and have her pack a bag."

He hung up.

Chapter 27

"We got Committees of Resistance formin' in Tennessee, Alabama, Pennsylvania, both Carolinas. We'll alert 'em all to keep their eyes peeled for your woman and kids, and that's a promise," Abner Fulsom stated emphatically. "Don't think we can't sympathize with y'all, cause we can. And don't y'all think we don't appreciate it, hear? I mean you and these other fellas helpin' us go up against them Reds—tough stuff, huh?"

Rourke remembered having met the man once some years back. He'd run a hardware store. The "Committee of Resistance" was some twenty men strong, at least this night, and their weapons ranged from the sublime to the ridiculous, Rourke thought, and everything in between. There were lever action .30-30 Winchesters, bolt action rifles of various persuasions, Colt, FN and Heckler & Koch assault type rifles and one or two sawn-back pump shotguns. Th⌐

149

handguns ranged from single-action Ruger Super Blackhawks in cowboy-style holsters to Walther PPK/S .380s to .45s to almost every imaginable Colt or Smith & Wesson revolver variant. One man had a MAC-10. He'd been a submachine gun collector before the war and had loaned or given away much of his collection to the Resistance. Unfortunately, Rourke thought, the people who had most of the selective fire weapons were somewhere else at the present.

"What about Colfax?" Reed asked.

"Yeah, but somethin' tells me, Captain, I'm gonna leave that information on where Jim Colfax is hangin' out 'til after tonight. You never know what might happen," Abner Fulsom said, smiling, his bright white teeth catching the light of the Coleman lamp.

"All right," Rourke said, tired of the talk, tired of the entire situation. "Where's the raid going to be, on what. What kind of resistance can we expect, how do we get there, you know, all that standard movie stuff, hmmm?"

Darren Ball, Rourke thought, had been strangely silent, sitting with an AR-15 across his lap and a Government Model .45 in a military type across the chest shoulder holster. Rourke thought Ball's silence wouldn't last for long.

Abner Fulsom began to speak. "There was a huge, modern shopping center not too far from the city—real popular place before the war. Russian occupation forces are usin' it now as a supply depot and helicopter base because of the big parking lot. Some of us blew up the airport when we learned the

Russians were comin' in, so they've been usin' the shopping center. There's a big ammo dump there, too. Figure we can steal all the AK-47s and such we can carry and ammo for them, blow up everything else. We go to the shopping center. We got a code name for it—Firehole.''

"Anything else?" Rourke asked.

"Yeah, we know a secret way into the place, too, through a big storm drain. It's still operational, but there hasn't been no big storm lately so the drain should be pretty dry. I figure—"

"That's all?" Rourke asked Fulsom.

"Yeah, about it. Why?"

"Well . . ." Rourke began slowly, then stopped, Darren Ball interrupting him.

"What he means is a commando type raid against a hardened military site like a supply depot isn't somethin' you whip up on the spur of the moment, Fulsom. Same thing I've been tryin' to tell you for a long time. That's why the last raid got you so many casualties.''

"What last raid?" Rourke asked.

"These damned fools," Ball began. "Aww—they decided to go and dynamite the guard posts in the center of town, blew up one part of the installation, killed maybe a half dozen Russian soldiers, and lost five of their own men.''

"How many men you have?" Rourke asked Fulsom.

"Well, we got a—"

"You ever use women?"

"Well, we always figured the women wasn't really good at—"

"Women do just as well in Resistance work as men—some of them are more savage fighters than a man could ever be," Rourke told the assembled Committee of Resistance. "You're cutting down your personnel pool by more than half that way. Women can get in places innocently where men can't—the whole thing. What explosives are you using for this raid?" Rourke asked, changing the subject.

"Well, we got a little dynamite. Figure to steal our explosives on the spot and take some extras along." Fulsom looked nervous for the first time.

Rourke shook his head, saying, "What if they're fresh out of explosives, what if they don't keep detonation devices anywhere nearby, what if—a whole bunch of what-ifs. This isn't a raid, its mass suicide. Count me out," Rourke said, unhooking his right thumb from the carry handle on the CAR-15 slung under his arm and wrapping his fist around the pistol grip. He turned to go back toward the tree line.

"Mr. Rourke?"

It was Fulsom's voice, and Rourke turned around. "What?"

"We need a raid like this. We need to show the Russians we can strike back and strike back hard. I got some dynamite. Maybe we can rig something. Maybe—"

"Hell." Rourke almost whispered, turning back toward the members of the Committee of Resistance. Like most committees generally, Rourke thought, it wasn't doing too well in the logic department.

Chapter 28

"I'm goin' with Pa to join up with the Resistance, and that's the plain fact," the red-haired boy said.

Sarah turned from watching the moon on the porch steps and looked at the boy, Thad, Mary's son. Sixteen, she guessed, give or take a year. Sarah turned and stared back at the moon, hugging her knees up to her, swatting at a mosquito against her bare calf and pulling her dress down lower over her legs.

"Thad, don't you think your mother needs a man around the house. Your father, your brothers— they're all in the Resistance." Inside, she could hear Michael and Annie running, playing, screaming with happiness.

"Sarah's right, boy, we need a man 'round here," Mary Mulliner said softly.

Sarah Rourke watched the sky, trying to pick the constellations of stars on the clear night air.

"Them Russians is buildin' a big fort or base near where Chattanooga used to be," the boy began again, his voice sounding artificially deepened.

"Chattanooga's still there, Thad," Sarah commented. "But all the people are dead. I don't think you'd want to see Chattanooga; there was death just everywhere." The thought of the neutron-bombed city—she assumed that had been what had happened—made her shiver. No men, no women, no children. The dogs, the cats, the birds, the grass was all brown and yellow, the trees were just there—but all dead. She shivered again. "You wouldn't want to see Chattanooga, Thad," Sarah said again.

"That big base the Russians is got," Thad insisted. "Gotta stop 'em before they get so all set up and everythin' they can't get stopped, you know."

The boy wanted reassurance, Sarah thought. She laughed—almost out loud. Men so often—at least some men—insisted women were so alike. Men were sometimes alike, too, she thought now, and she almost envied it. If John, her husband, were still alive—she wanted him to be—whatever John was doing now, he was consumed with it, she was sure. He was searching for her, searching for the children, fighting Communist soldiers perhaps, brigands very likely. Men found "toys" for their minds even under the worst circumstances, just from their role of being men. There was always something to do, to go up against.

She leaned against the post beside the porch railing and stared out across the dark expanse of the fields. Thad and her husband, John—their thing to do now was go and fight. Mary and herself, too, if she found John (*when,* she reminded herself, or when he found her). She would wait, care for the children, keep the home, clean the wounds, and go quietly insane each time she thought of John going out and perhaps dying. She stared up at the peculiar haze around the moon, wishing John were there to tell her what it meant. Was the world ending—the heat, the cold, the torrential rains, the red sunsets?

"Mary," she said, her voice trembling slightly. "Mary, I'm going to leave in a few days because if I don't—" she stood up and walked into the darkness, wishing she had a sweater, cold suddenly.

"If I don't," she whispered to herself and the night, "I won't have the strength to do anything, but stay here."

Chapter 29

Col. Vassily Korcinski hung up the radio telephone. He walked from his desk to the small mirror inside the open closet door, smoothed his white hair with his hands, and studied his face. Classic, he thought, chiseled. He couldn't help but smile. Other than his own image, he thought, he was pleased that Varakov trusted him so.

He walked back to his desk, lifted the red telephone to his day room and waited. It rang less than once. A voice answered with the formal identification of place, rank and last name, and the inevitable "Sir!"

He cut the man off. "This is Colonel Korcinski. Alert the counter-terrorist force to move out within five minutes."

Korcinski hung up the telephone, walked back to the closeted mirror and took his cap, adjusting it at a slight angle over his left eye, smoothing back the white hair, smoothing his uniform jacket under the gunbelt, opening the flap holster, working the slide on the pistol and chambering the first round, then setting the Makarov's safety, the hammer down. Reholstering the gun, glancing once more into the mirror, he closed the closet door and started across his office.

As he opened the door into the hall, the sirens began sounding. He strode purposefully—he was conscious of himself and had always been—down the hallway, the sounds of running feet in the hallway of the journalism building and now his staff headquarters reassuring to him.

Narcissism, some called it that. He called it pride and realization of his destiny. He turned the corner into the side corridor, the glassed wall on one side looking out into the central square where the counter-terrorist force was already forming. He walked along the hallway, staring into the glass, seeing his own image half-reflected and superimposed on the glass over the figures of running armed men, motorcycle units, and troop vehicles. He walked to the end of the hallway and through the glass doors, adjusting his hat to a bit more rakish angle in the reflection, then started down the steps, his boots gleaming in the reflected artificial lighting.

He reached the base of the steps, turned left, pushed briskly through the double-glass doors, and took one last glance. He stepped out onto the brick porch and walked down its length, surveying the men, the officers saluting as he passed. Korcinski returned the salutes with a studied casualness. He could see his aide running up to him, bringing his

157

greatcoat and his swagger stick. He stopped, letting the man hold the coat for him. Korcincski left the collar up, the coat hanging open, the swagger stick under his left arm as he pulled the skin-tight leather gloves over his manicured fingers.

He slapped the swagger stick against his right thigh, glancing with great drama at the watch on his wrist. It was only four minutes, and the men were already assembled, the troops boarded into the trucks, the motorcycle patrols mounted, his staff car waiting.

He stepped to the edge of the porch, speaking at the top of his voice, carefully listening to it for the tone, the life in it. He liked the way it resonated through the square, the stone buildings making it reverberate as though he were speaking from some far loftier height.

"We have been notified of a full-scale terrorist assault to be conducted at a location not far from here." He liked to preserve an element of mystery, the very ambiguity he'd learned to imbue his men with a sense of the importance of it all. "We are to contain the terrorists until their ammunition is exhausted, then to take them in hand-to-hand combat and preserve as many of their lives as possible. There is one man—he is tall, his hair is dark, rising from a high forehead, he frequently wears sunglasses even at night—he will be wearing several handguns and be skilled in their use. No one man is to attempt to take him—squad action only. If any man kills this man, he will himself be shot. This man, at all costs, must be taken alive and as uninjured as possible. I can explain no further for reasons of security. We will move out toward the helicopter staging area and supply depot.''

He stood then, quietly, surveying the faces of his men, then shouted, ''We toil for the liberation of the workers of the world, and for this reason we ourselves are invincible!''

A cheer—spontaneous he thought—went up from the assembled troops and he waved the swagger stick in his gloved hands. He had always admired the incantation the Nazis had used: spirit was important. He saluted the swagger stick against the peak of his hat and strode toward the steps at the far side of the brick porch leading down to his men, his staff car,—and to his destiny.

Chapter 30

Rourke stared at the moon and the curious, ghostlike haze around it. He shuddered slightly. The night was cold, the air here on the river was damp and chill, but the shudder was for some other reason he couldn't quite define. He glanced skyward at the haloed moon. The shudder came again and he knew why.

The water of the river made tiny, wavelike lapping sounds against the hull of the rubber boat as in silence and darkness Rourke's boat and three more similar to it stayed to the middle of the river, searching the blackness and shadow on the right bank for the outlet of the storm drain. In the darkness, he felt the safety on the CAR-15, checked the security of the twin stainless Detonics pistols in their shoulder holsters, checked the security of the flap on the Ranger rig holding the Metalifed Government .45 on his hip. He forced himself to slow his breathing. He was nervous; the mission held something that smelled bad to him, tasted foul. There was something very wrong with it, and it wasn't just the poor planning or the inexperienced people. He half-wished Paul Rubenstein had been well enough to come along. At least he trusted Paul, and for what Paul lacked in experience, he compensated well in intelligence and initiative.

Rourke pulled up the collar of his leather jacket, snapping closed the second highest button on the off-white cowboy shirt he wore beneath it. He snatched off the sunglasses, securing them in his shirt pocket, squinting as his eyes adjusted to the difference in light. He almost laughed aloud; if he hadn't been so sensitive to light all through his life, he would have thought it symptomatic of radiation sickness. He checked the closure on the canvas musette bag hanging from his left side over the M-16 Bayonet, the closure on the Bushnell Armored 8 x 30s hanging from his right side. The bottoms of his jeans were rolled in with blousing garters over the tops of his combat boots—stuffing the pants in the boots had always been uncomfortable to him. He remembered once, years earlier, having fought his way five miles in subfreezing temperatures through more than two feet of fresh snow on foot—the drifts had been as high as his thighs and he had fallen several times—then the pants had been tucked into the boots to keep the snow out. He had made it then and he thought that somehow he'd make it tonight. He had to. He had come to think of it as a quest—no less important than a search for the Grail, for any treasure ancient or modern—more important because it was a human quest, to find the three surviving humans who meant the most to him in all the world, the woman he had always loved, the son, the daughter—each child part of him and part of her.

"Over there, past those rocks and weeds," Rourke heard Fulsom rasp. Rourke shook his head, searching out Fulsom in the darkness, finding his silhouette, and then seeing in what direction the man pointed.

Rourke, his night vision better than most because of light sensitivity, could see the outline of the upper right quarter of the storm drain's circular entrance clearly. Rats, snakes, wolf spiders possibly—he set his jaw, staring at the entrance as two of Reed's men, doing the rowing on Rourke's boat, changed course from the center of the river toward the marshy, muddy bank.

As the rubber boat skidded into the mud, Rourke was already on his feet and going over the gunwales, the sounds of critters on the land and things in the water something he listened intently for.

Rourke approached the storm drain entrance, Reed beside him and Fulsom behind Reed. Rourke glanced back toward the entrance.

"What the hell is that?" Reed whispered, pointing toward a silver glinting sphere from something reminiscent of thread.

"It's a spider nest. See 'em in trees and branches a lot."

"Hell," Reed rasped, starting to take the bayonet from his belt and hack at the nest.

Rourke caught his wrist, looking at him hard in the moonlight. "If it were blocking the entrance, fine, if it were in our way, fine—never kill anything unless you have to—there're enough things you have to kill these days."

Rourke sidestepped in front of Reed and glanced around him, then took his Zippo and flicked it lit, lighting one of his small, dark cigars, and glanced at the luminous face of the Rolex on his wrist in the light of the flame, then moved the blue-yellow fire toward the entrance, up and down and from side to side, inspecting the tunnel beyond the lip of the storm drain.

"What do you think, Mr. Rourke?" Fulsom asked, his voice low beside Rourke.

"My first name is John. What do I think about the storm drain? Maybe a nice place to visit, but . . ." Rourke let the sentence hang, his gloved left hand pushing away cobwebs at the top of the storm drain as he ducked his head to step inside.

He could feel his feet squishing the mud in the darkness. He closed the Zippo and reached into his belt under his leather jacket, snatching the Safariland Kel-Lite and pushing the switch forward with his thumb. As the light filled the storm drain, he could see it glinting on what looked to him like eyes beyond the light and in the shadow ahead, he could hear scurrying and the high-pitched scratchiness of bats.

"What the hell is that?" Reed asked, suddenly beside Rourke, stooped slightly as Rourke was.

Rourke started to answer, but Fulsom, there too, said, "Bats I think."

"Bats!"

"They're small—not the vampire kind. If you

were a peach or a pear you'd be in trouble." Rourke added.

"Whew! That's a relief," Reed muttered.

"Yeah," Rourke told him. "Just don't let 'em scratch you or bite. They carry rabies sometimes." Rourke started forward, hearing the shuffling of feet behind him from the rest of the sixteen man commando force. Two of Reed's men and some of Fulsom's—including Darren Ball—were waiting with the boats.

"Bats! God, betcha there're snakes, too," Reed muttered.

"Most poisonous snakes won't kill you, just make you damned sick—unless you have a reaction to the venom," Rourke consoled Reed, flashing his light ahead across the reddish brown mud, swatting at cobwebs with his free right hand, the CAR-15 slung across his back, muzzle down.

The storm drain's height was six feet, the diameter, and there was a simple choice Rourke decided—either walk through the deepest and slipperiest of the squishing mud and duck your head a little or walk to the side on angle and move half-stooped. He chose the muddy water and mire.

Shuffling along through the storm drain with Rourke's flashlight and two others at intervals along the seventeen man single-file column the only illumination, Rourke paced himself, trying to judge the distance, not trusting wholly what Fulsom had described as a mile's walk. A rat scurried across Rourke's left foot as the tunnel the drain formed took a slight bend along an elbow of pipe then curved at a right angle, then started slightly upward.

Rourke stopped, his light hitting a swarm of bats hanging from the top of the drain, ducking as they whistled and whined overhead, one of the men screaming, Reed starting to bring his M-16 to bear and Rourke swatting it down, but saying nothing. They moved on, roaches everywhere on the floor of the drain near the edge of the mire, feeding on the bat droppings, perhaps, Rourke thought.

After several more minutes, Rourke stopped, flashing his light behind him, searching for Fulsom's face, seeing the terror in the eyes. Abner Fulsom said, "I'm a little claustrophobic. Place gives me the creeps."

"I don't think anybody exactly likes it," Rourke almost whispered. "I make it we've done a mile—no end of the tunnel is in sight. How much further?"

"My brother laid the drain, told me about it—said it was just about an even mile."

"And it lets out in a small culvert at the edge of the parking lot, then dips back under the lot toward the shopping center itself?"

"Yeah, that's what he said," Fulsom whispered.

"Where's your brother now?" Rourke snapped.

"Dead. He was in Atlanta when the bombs or missiles or whatever hit it—"

Rourke exhaled hard. "I'm sorry." He turned and shone his Kel-Lite back along the storm drain. Without saying anything else, he started walking again. If Fulsom's memory were correct, Rourke judged, then the culvert should be coming up soon. He swung the CAR-15 from his back, slinging it under his right arm, suspended from his right shoulder, his fist wrapped around the pistol grip.

After another five minutes, Rourke stopped, cutting the light.

"Back flat against the wall," he rasped, then started edging forward. There was light—dim—but light none the less, up ahead. He moved toward it. The smell in the drain had been bad, but here it was worse, the drain partially clogged and the water several inches deep. He edged up along the side and stooped as he went forward, grateful for the insect repellant he had used. There were swarms of small flies and mosquitoes, some of them, he wagered with himself, carried sleeping sickness.

The tunnel took a slight bend around a right-angle elbow joint, and Rourke stopped again at the mouth of the tunnel, a heavy-looking grillwork over the drain opening beyond and a V-shaped cement culvert visible in the moonlight ahead.

Rourke moved as silently as he could toward the grating, peering beyond it into the open, smelling the comparatively fresh night air, breathing it in deeply. The grille was set into the mouth of the drain, forming a grid of squares eight inches roughly on each side, a thin layer of cement holding it in place, a slightly wider opening at the top and bottom and each side where the grid of steel didn't quite fit—an afterthought, he guessed.

Rourke heard no noise outside—nothing. The quiet seemed ominous to him. He edged back into the drain, taking a deep breath of the fresher air before he did. He stopped where Reed, Fulsom, and the others crouched along the side of the drain beyond the elbow.

"I need a couple of bayonets and a couple of

good-sized rocks. Going to have to hammer our way out."

"Why don't you use that bayonet you got," Reed snapped.

"I paid for mine—yours is issue—we'll use yours," Rourke told him quietly. "And let's get going. Time's against us." Rourke glanced at his watch. It was just past midnight, and they still hadn't even penetrated the base.

Reed barked an order to one of his two men and after a moment, two bayonets and two paving bricks were handed up along the line. "Come on," Rourke said, distributing one set of the tools to Reed.

With the Intelligence captain behind him, Rourke started forward again toward the elbow, through it and then, slowly, toward the grating at the end of the storm drain. Reed started to chisel at the cement and Rourke stopped him, raising a finger to his lips for silence and listening to the night sounds and listening for some sign of activity by the Russians. It was as if the place were deserted, Rourke thought, and that was all wrong. He was tempted to turn back, but realized then that any chance of the Resistance people or the Army Intelligence people helping to find Sarah and the children would be gone. Pausing for another moment, swinging the CAR-15 out of the way, Rourke set the point of one of the borrowed bayonets to the bead of cement and drew back the paving brick in his right hand.

"Watch your eyes for chips," Rourke cautioned Reed, then smashed the paving brick down against the butt of the bayonet, a two-inch fragment of the cement bead breaking way and falling into the muddy water in which they stood. In an instant, Reed was chiseling away at the opposite side.

"Cheap construction," Rourke thought, a six- or seven-inch piece of the cement bead chipping under the impact of his blow. It took both men some ten minutes to get a sufficient amount of the cement chipped away to try pushing at the grating. It budged, but didn't give way. They resumed chiseling at the cement, then when the cement was nearly gone from both sides, threw their weight against the grating a second time. This time it moved and slipped too easily. Rourke and Reed frantically caught at it to avoid letting it fall and clang against the cement of the V-shaped channel in the culvert outside. They edged the grating along the side of the storm drain, conscious of every clang and scrape. Rourke sent Reed back to get Fulsom and the others, Rourke himself moving out of the storm drain, up the side of the channel and peered over the edge of the culvert and across. The parking lot was comparatively huge for a largely rural area, the yellow lines drawn for orderly parking meaningless now. A few rusted wrecks sat in the lot at the far side, but that was all. Closer in, toward the shopping center itself, Rourke could see Soviet-marked trucks—the Red Stars seeming to burn in the night, somehow, psychological he imagined.

"What's up?"

Rourke turned toward the voice: it was Reed.

"You've been around," Rourke rasped, slipping down from the edge of the culvert, leaning back against the steeply sloping cement behind him. "This whole deal smells. We're not going in the rest of the way through the storm drain; we're cutting across this lot and into the buildings. There's a trap out there. Only thing we can do is try and work around it."

"Fulsom's not gonna like that," Reed cautioned.

"Yeah, well—that's too damned bad," Rourke said. "I'll let him lead the war when he lets me sell hardware. Come on."

Slipping back toward the mouth of the storm drain, Rourke put his left hand on Fulsom's shoulder and drew the man aside, telling him, "There's some kind of trap in the wind. I can feel it. We're going through the parking area, to the buildings. Couple of us go up on the roofs after sentries, then everybody piles after us. If it looks possible, some of us can go into the complex through the roof."

"But why not the drain, the way we had—"

"You want to go that route, count me out," Rourke rasped.

Fulsom, the corners of his mouth set down hard, nodded—grim-looking, Rourke thought.

"All right, you keep a handle on things here," Rourke said. "I'll take Reed and his two Army Intelligence guys with me."

Edging back toward the lip of the culvert up the V-shaped channel, he waved toward Reed, the Intelligence captain moving diagonally along the rough concrete surface toward him.

"Get your two boys, then stay with me," Rourke told him emotionlessly. "First shot or anything from us or them, get the hell out. Pass that back along to Fulsom." Rourke snatched the Bushnell Armored binoculars from their case and scanned the parking area, then the roof tops. He assumed there would naturally be sentries though he saw none. Shaking his head as he replaced the glasses, he zipped his jacket against the night air, but the cold feeling in his stomach wouldn't go.

Chapter 31

"These are the complete details of your architectural survey, Lieutenant?"

"Yes, Comrade Colonel," the ruddy cheeked young man said, still standing at attention beside the open door leading to the back seat of Colonel Korcinski's staff car.

"Excellent. This storm drain, it appears here." He showed the page of the plans through the open door. The lieutenant bent over formally, studying them by the beam from the flashlight Korcinski held in his gloved left hand.

"Yes, Comrade Colonel?"

"You will be commander for this portion of the operation. Do not fail. Take a platoon of men to the outlet of this storm drain, approach with caution, apprehend any persons near or inside the outlet of the drain, then proceed up the drain pipe toward the parking square. Any questions?"

"All is clear, Comrade Colonel!"

"Excellent. Get moving," Korcinski snapped, tempering his tone of authority with one he thought of encouragement.

Korcinski turned to the captain, who had been standing beside the young lieutenant. "I understand this man Rourke that we seek is highly experienced. He will no doubt become alarmed that there is no visible presence in the parking square or on the roof tops. I doubt he will proceed along the storm drain past this point." The captain bent toward the page of the survey Korcinski held under the flashlight. "This is some sort of opening. You will position men at the far boundary of the parking square in case Rourke and these others decide to withdraw. Otherwise, if you make contact, keep them under direct observation, but do nothing. Maintain radio silence in the event they are tuned to our usual frequencies. The jaws of the trap will close when they enter the complex or if they try to escape. Remember, Captain. Take this one Rourke alive. Preserve his weapons. He is not to be harmed."

"Comrade Colonel?" the captain asked.

Anticipating the captain, Korcinski said," I cannot confide this reasoning to you. It is at the highest levels of security." As the captain started to go, Korcinski added, "Has the plane arrived yet from Chicago?"

"Yes, Comrade Colonel, moments ago."

"Very good. The young woman aboard is to be brought here and kept safely away from any of the fighting; she is not to be questioned."

"Yes, Comrade Colonel."

Lazily—a studied movement—Korcinski returned the salute. He could not tell the captain why this man Rourke was to be taken unharmed, his weapons kept. He had not been told himself. He studied his reflection in the glass as his driver closed the open rear passenger door and the light from one of the motorcycles in the escort hit the tinted glass just right.

Chapter 32

Rourke pushed himself up and raced from the lip of the culvert and across the parking lot toward the grassy knoll some two hundred yards away, the CAR-15 in his right fist, the safety off, the freshness of the air exhilarating to his lungs, his hair blowing across his face and then back from his forehead in the cool night wind. He hit the grassy knoll and threw himself to the ground, hugging the green as he waited for Reed, then the two men after him. Sighting through the Colt's three-power scope, he tried spotting the roof line. Again he saw nothing, then edged along the grass closer toward the building, Reed was nearly across the parking area now, one of the other men already starting out from the culvert.

Rourke stopped, rolling onto his back on the grass, catching his breath, staring up at the night sky and the stars. The haze was still around the moon and it wasn't the moon, Rourke knew, but something in the atmosphere. He snatched a tuft of grass from beside him—it was green and healthy—he could feel a mist starting to fall. Was the rain radioactive yet? he wondered. There was so little time for him to find Sarah and the children, if there were any time at all. There was safety in the retreat. He stared up as the stars began fading above a thin layer of clouds. What then, he asked himself, what after he found Sarah, Michael, Ann? Life in the retreat forever, go outside specially suited-up because the air was foul? What if radiation seeped through the ground into the water source for the retreat somewhere hundreds of miles away? He monitored and tested the water periodically—but what if? The ifs were gnawing at him; he had no choice but to find his family, and after that somehow keep them all alive. And what if between the time from when he had found the tracks and now they had died? What if they thought he were dead?

Doubt, he thought, doubt . . .

"See anything?"

He glanced to his left, a part of his consciousness noticing Reed edging up along side him.

"No—nothing," Rourke muttered, watching across the parking area as the last man began his headlong lunge across the open area—a target, but Rourke doubted anyone would shoot. He was convinced now that the Communists were setting a trap, and what drew him on, he supposed, was the reason behind it. If they wanted the attackers in the commando team dead, they would have opened up already, sealed the storm drain, potshotted them through the other side or gassed them; there were an infinite number of ways to kill.

Whatever the trap, it was important enough to risk the supply depot and the helicopter landing field on the other side of the shopping center. Whatever the trap, the mass death of the commando team was not its objective. Rourke's stomach turned and his palms began to sweat under the gloves he wore.

The last of Reed's two men hit the grassy area and Rourke waited a moment for the corporal to catch his breath, then signaled Reed and the two men to move out, edging along the ground on his hands and knees toward the rise at the top of the knoll, keeping his head below it and peering beyond. There was more of the parking area, where he finally saw some signs of life—but not enough, he told himself. There were two fixed-wing aircraft of the single-engine variety, apparently used for observation flights, and with a short enough takeoff that they could use the lot. Trucks were parked alongside the buildings and there were lights from inside through what had once been the windows of the stores when it had still been a shopping center.

Rourke dropped below the edge and turned toward Reed, close behind him. "I make it about six feet to the nearest part of that lower level roof line, six feet from the grass. Let's get everybody up and over except that corporal. Have him wait five minutes in case some shooting starts. No sense getting more people killed than we have to."

Rourke didn't wait for a reply, but started moving, running in a low crouch toward the nearest roof line, setting his safety on and letting the rifle sling back behind his shoulder, upping his speed, raising to his full height as he ran the last few yards, his hands going out ahead of him, his feet coming together as he forced himself up, his hands clawing for the roof line, then getting a grip and pulling his body up and over. On his hands and knees, pushing himself up to a crouch, he swung the rifle forward, edging off the safety, making a quick visual inspection of the scope, ascertaining there was no damage and moving off toward what apparently was a roof-mounted air conditioner. Going flat against it, he surveyed the roof line: it was a trap. He was certain now there were no guards. He could see men on the next higher roof level, but only a fool of a commander would have left an entire section of the roof line unguarded.

He glanced behind him, seeing Reed coming over the roof line and almost immediately after him one of the two men with him. Rourke signaled Reed and the other man to follow him, then ducked from behind the air-conditioning unit to the edge of the higher roof line, going into a crouch. Reed joined him.

"There—that's why it's a trap," Rourke rasped, jabbing his thumb toward the guards on the next roof line. "Wait a minute, take this." Rourke slipped the safety on his CAR-15 and pushed himself up the six feet to the next roof line, scrambling over it and dropping flat against the tarred surface. He studied the guard nearest him, one man, standing in the open—an obvious setup, he thought.

Rourke crawled on his stomach along the roof surface toward the side overlooking the knoll.

Peering over the edge, he saw something that, though he expected it, made his blood run cold—a large concentration of troops waiting in the wooded areas beyond the far side of the upper-level parking area. He ducked down, then, running in a low crouch, crossed the roof line to the far parking areas in front of the shopping center. Rourke dropped low beside the roof edge and looked over the side—Soviet armor surrounded the several dozen military helicopters on the ground, motorcycle-mounted troops ringing what looked to be a staff car.

"Shit!" Rourke muttered, then started back toward Reed and reached the roof edge and flipping over the side, dropping and flexing his knees to break the fall.

"Well?"

"Well, kiss your fanny good-bye," Rourke snapped, starting toward the roof line fronting the knoll.

The corporal was just coming over the roof line. Rourke caught the man in his arms against his chest, breaking his fall and turning him around. "Back down, Corporal," Rourke snapped, hitting the roof edge and flipping down on the grass, rolling and tumbling down the knoll, coming up on his knees, the CAR-15 at his hip.

"Come on!" he snapped, breaking into a deadrun across the parking lot. The trap was about to spring, he thought, and there was too much of it to wait it out. There wasn't even time to run.

Rourke saw someone coming up over the lip of the culvert. Fulsom? The man's arms were waving. He was choking, it looked like, his body doubling over, the knees buckling, then the man pushed himself up and ran toward them again. Rourke glanced behind him. First was the corporal, then Reed, then the other soldier.

Fulsom was shouting something and Rourke tried waving him down, signaling him to be still. But Fulsom was still shouting. Rourke couldn't make out the words, but heard the spasms of coughing. Rourke glanced behind him again; the lower roof was swarming now with Soviet troops, and the upper-level parking area was no longer nearly deserted. He could see the canvas roof lines of Soviet military trucks there. In the distance, from the other side of the shopping center, he could make out the revving of motorcycle engines. Rourke could hear Fulsom now, the words still cluttered sounding from the coughing, "Gas! They got all of—" Then Fulsom dropped, a single rifle shot echoing in the night.

Rourke stopped running, looked up at the roof, saw a Soviet trooper, an officer beside him jerking him around, slapping him in the face.

There was a bullhorn—the English very good—the words; "Lay down your weapons and you will be unharmed!"

Rourke snatched the CAR-15 to his shoulder, telescoping the stock, his eye picking up the rifleman who'd triggered the shot from the roof, the crosshairs of the three-power scope settling across the helmeted head, Rourke's trigger finger twitching once, the single 5.56mm rifle bullet's noise as it crossed the air to its target like a thunderclap in the otherwise total silence.

The soldier stumbled back, then fell forward over the roof line to the loading dock below.

Rourke stood, motionless, the rifle still shouldered, waiting. He might be done, he knew, there were too many of them. He settled the crosshairs on the officer who only a second earlier had stood beside the now-dead Russian soldier.

The bullhorn sounded again, "Lay down your arms and you will not be harmed!"

Rourke scanned the roof line for the bullhorn, spotted it, and fired. The bullhorn shattered from the hand of the man, the white metal thing falling from sight.

At the top of his voice, the rifle in front of his chest at high port, Rourke shouted, "Bite my ass!" Then he started to run.

Chapter 33

Colonel Korcinski shouted to his driver, "Stop! There he is!" And before the car had settled, he was opening the rear passenger door, then stepped out into the parking lot.

He could see the man he wanted. It had to be Rourke, tall, lean, a brown leather jacket, a rifle in his hands, his hair blowing in the wind as he ran. The light mist that Korcinski had noted earlier on the windshield was turning into a steady slow rain and, ignoring it, he started walking forward, shouting to the leader of the motorcycle detachment, "Get that man—alive—the others be damned! Get that man Rourke!"

Then, turning to the driver standing beside him now, he snapped, "Field glasses!" In a moment his chauffeur had returned and Korcinski had the glasses up to his eyes and was adjusting them. He watched Rourke running and shooting, the troopers swarming toward him not returning fire as they closed in, crumpling under the withering accuracy of his bullets.

Rourke made to fire the rifle; it was apparently empty. Three of Korcinski's soldiers were closing on him, then suddenly one went down, and there was a rumbling sound from a heavy-caliber weapon. There was a pistol in Rourke's right hand, dully gleaming in the spotlights from the trucks, belching fire against the darkness behind him, then firing again. Two more of Korcinski's men went down. And Rourke was running again.

"Get him! That man must be stopped." He was tempted, sorely tempted, he realized, to disobey his direct orders, and order his men to shoot rather than get cut down by this American who was somehow so important to General Varakov. Mentally, he bit his tongue, shouting, "Get that man—but do not under any circumstances harm him. Get him!"

Chapter 34

A motorcyclist was closing in on him. Rourke sidestepped and, as the cyclist missed him by a good two feet, Rourke swung the CAR-15 from the muzzle like a baseball bat, notching the Soviet motorcyclist on the chin and knocking him from the bike. The bike rolled ahead a few yards and spun out.

Rourke snatched a fresh thirty-round magazine for the CAR-15 and rammed it home, shoving the empty in his belt, holstering the Colt .45 Automatic as he ran for the bike, wrestling the bike up and kick-starting it, still settling himself across it as the wheels were already beginning to move.

The CAR-15 slung from his right shoulder and out of the way, Rourke revved the bike, taking it in a wide circle as other Soviet motorcycle troopers started toward him, closing in.

He caught a glimpse of a man standing by the staff car he'd seen earlier, but now on this side of the parking lot, field glasses in front of his face.

"I'll give you a good show, pal," Rourke muttered to himself, getting the RPMs up on the Soviet motorcycle and turning off sharply left, heading toward the green of the grassy knoll on the far side of the lot. He hadn't done the hell-for-leather kind of hill climbing for years, he thought, his hands like vises on the bike, getting every ounce from the gears that he could as he bent low over the machine for the run toward the knoll, then reaching up as he hit the incline, swaying his balance from side to side, his feet going out, supporting him, then pulling up, skittering along over the grass as he jumped the lip of concrete onto the upper-level parking lot. More of the motorcycle troopers were there, and trucks loaded with troops, the men spilling from them and swarming toward him. Rourke curved the bike, slowing it, firing the CAR-15 across his body at them, then letting the rifle hang at his side, revving the bike, going low over the handlebars. He started toward the knoll again. There were as many as a dozen of the Soviet motorcycle troopers starting up the knoll toward him, and Rourke cut his wheel left, veering away from the knoll, exited from the parking lot blocked by trucks at the far end. A cloud of orange rolled toward him, and he glanced from side to side. Most of the Soviet troopers were wearing gas masks.

He veered the bike left, a line of six Soviet cyclists coming toward him, the CAR-15 in his hand, firing, like knights he thought, jousting, but with guns rather than lances.

Two of the Soviet troopers went down and he

fired again, cutting his power, grinding the bike to a halt, bending low over one of the dead soldiers, snatching the gas mask from the dead man's face, pulling it in place over his own face, then he jumped back on the motorcycle and started back toward the knoll.

The orange cloud was rolling toward him, obscuring his view. He angled the bike away from it and across the parking lot, a dozen bikers coming in single rank at speed toward him. He veered the bike left again and toward the knoll.

Flattening himself, low over the handlebars, the wind whistling across the gas mask making a howling sound in his ears, the throb of the motor between his legs shuddered through his frame.

Six of the Soviet motorcycle troopers, just below the lip of the knoll—Rourke couldn't stop, revved the bike and jumped it, soaring out over their heads, the bike landing hard, shuddering under him, the front wheel not reacting to his hands, the bike skidding away from him, Rourke spilling from it, slithering across the parking lot surface, his face numbed on the left side. His left arm pained him, the CAR-15 was gone from his shoulder.

Rourke tried to push himself up as he ripped away the gas mask. He couldn't get past his knees, a dozen of the Soviet foot soldiers now rushed him, the Colt Goernment .45 coming into his right hand, spitting all the death he could muster, his left hand snatching the Detonics under his right arm, the hammer jerking back under his thumb, the stainless .45 bucking in his hand as he pumped the trigger.

The Colt fell from his right fist, empty. And he

185

snatched the second Detonics, firing it point blank into the first wave of the Soviet soldiers.

They were falling, but the gun in his left hand was empty. He fired the last round from the Detonics in his right hand, then spun the pistol on the trigger guard, hammering the butt down on the face of the neaest of the Soviet troopers, his left hand snatching the M-16 bayonet from his belt, driving it forward into one of the Russians, catching it into the throat and ripping, then drawing it out, the blood-tinged Parkerized blade ramming forward into another of the soldier's midsection. The Detonics gone from his right hand, Rourke staggered to his feet, the A.G. Russell Sting IA in his right hand, slashing.

There was a ring of men around him now and a knife in each of his hands. "You want me alive," Rourke snapped, "then pay for it!" The soldiers closed on him, Rourke's hands and arms working like pistons, driving the knife blades, slashing. Men fell, stumbling and dying around him. The bayonet was gone, stuck in somebody's chest, and he swung the Sting IA in a wide arc, the Soviet soldiers edging away as Rourke spun in a circle with the knife outstretched, the men closing again. He rammed the knife into somebody's stomach and tried getting it out. His right arm went numb as a rifle butt crashed down on it. He snatched at the nearest man, his left hand going for the throat, his fist tightening on the front of it and crushing the windpipe, his right knee driving upward into another man's groin, his right arm, still numb, swinging in front of him.

Someone had him around the knees, and Rourke hammered his left fist down in what, as a kid, he'd thought was a dirty rabbit punch. The pressure around his knees relaxed and Rourke threw his left fist forward, his knuckles splitting as he smashed out somebody's teeth, his numb right arm pushing away a snarling face inches from his, his left knee ramming into another man's groin.

Rourke started to fall back, kicking now as his feet went out from under him. A foot kicked into the side of his head; unconsciousness started to wash over him. He spotted the Sting IA on the ground, snatched at it and rammed it straight up, the blade hammering into the mouth of the man nearest him, blood spraying across Rourke's face, angry shouts from the men around him. Rourke started pushing himself up as the knot of soldiers pulled back for an instant, then he turned. There was a rifle butt coming at him and he ducked, throwing his head into the stomach of the man to his left, knocking the Soviet trooper to the ground, then feeling the pressure of bodies on top of him. The soldier beneath Rourke was screaming, Rourke's left hand knotted on the man's face, twisting at it, gouging.

Rourke rolled, several of the soldiers still clinging to him. He tried to push himself up. A tall man hurtled at Rourke and Rourke sprawled back.

Suddenly, it was Rourke and the tall soldier, everyone else backed away in a tight circle. The man's face was bloodied, his voice taut with emotion, his English bad, but intelligible. "I cannot kill you. I beat you though."

Rourke edged back a step, the soldier coming at him in a rush, Rourke sidestepping, his right foot coming up, the toe smashing into the soldier's groin, then the knee hammering upward into the soldier's jaw, missing the mouth. Rourke stumbled back. Someone behind him threw him forward.

The big Russian was up, his mouth bleeding heavily, his fists raised almost like a nineteenth-century pugilist. Rourke started for him, but the Russian's left fist smashed forward, catching Rourke on the right side of the head, the blow stunning him. The Russian dropped his guard and moved in. Rourke thought the Russian shouldn't have done that.

Rourke's left foot smashed upward, the upper part of his foot connecting square into the Russian's groin. The big man's black eyes bulged, his body stumbling forward as he doubled over. Both Rourke's fists doubled together and swung down across the man's exposed neck. The Russian fell. The soldiers ringed around Rourke, closing in, then suddenly parting in a wave to his right.

Fulsom's face, his shoulder a mass of blood, but he was alive. Beside him was the man Rourke had seen with the binoculars, the officer holding a pistol in his gloved right hand, the binoculars swinging almost lazily from his neck like a tourist. The muzzle of the pistol was flush against Fulsom's right temple.

"Rourke, stop or I fire. You understand?"

Rourke glared at the man, then saw the hammer drawn back under the officer's thumb.

"Your round," Rourke almost whispered, shaking his aching head to clear it.

Chapter 35

"You didn't have to do that, Rourke. Maybe you could have—"

"Would it do any good," Rourke said, "if I told you a hardware store owner once saved my life?"

Fulsom forced a smile, and Rourke clapped the man on the back, then tried looking through the crack in the canvas covering the back of the truck. They were heading into the woods on the far side of the city. Rourke anticipated the reason, but failed to see the logic. If they were planning a mass execution, why the harmless gas that had merely knocked out the men in the storm drain, why the kid-glove treatment of the men guarding the boats at the entrance to the storm drain, why the careful bandaging of Fulsom's shoulder and the antiseptic swabbing of the skinned left side of Rourke's face?

Why?

The truck stopped and, after a second Korcinski's

189

face appeared at the rear of the truck, a smile on his lips. He had even introduced himself to Rourke.

"Mr. Rourke, you only please, the others will be unharmed. And please, no more messy fist fights, hmm?"

Rourke shrugged, climbed past Fulsom, then over the tailgate at the rear of the truck and dropped down to the ground. Reed had been silent during the long ride, like Rourke, he assumed, mystified.

It was raining more heavily now.

Rourke, walking beside Korcinski, said, "Your English is good for a military man."

Korcinski doffed a salute, saying, "Thank you. I understand you have been a writer. I appreciate such a compliment. You are a trained physician too, are you not?"

"Yeah—although lately I've been doing less healing and more wounding."

Korcinski laughed, then outstretched his gloved right hand to Rourke's left forearm.

"Ivon," Korcinski snapped and a young soldier came forward, his arms laden with Rourke's guns.

"What the hell is—"

"Please, Mr. Rourke—please," Korcinski said. "Your weapons have been reloaded for you, checked for their functional reliability. I understand you may need them."

"You setting me up?" Rourke whispered.

"Hardly, just watching for your interests. The assault rifle was uninjured when it dropped. American guns I have always found to be sturdily built. Take them please."

Rourke took the twin Detonics pistols, shoving

them into his belt, then taking the Colt Government .45. The finish was unscratched despite the drop. He checked the Metalifed pistol: it was loaded, the chamber empty. He looked at Korcinski then at the gun. The man nodded and Rourke worked the slide, chambering a round, then lowering the hammer and holstering it. He'd looked by the glare of the headlights and the firing pin seemed in place as he held the gun awkwardly low while working the slide.

He did the same with each of the Detonics pistols and reinserted them in the shoulder holsters under his arms. The bayonet and the A.G. Russell knife were cleaned and oiled. He holstered them. "We took the liberty of reloading your spent magazine for the rifle. I'm afraid we had no American pistol ammunition available for your handgun."

"I'll let it slide," Rourke whispered.

He took the CAR-15. It was unscratched, the scope intact. He watched two guards standing off at a distance twitch as he telescoped the stock and shouldered the rife to check the scope, then replaced the scope covers, recollapsing the stock.

"We found your motorcycle not far from the drive-in theater, Mr. Rourke. We assumed at least it was yours. It is waiting here for you."

"How did you know about the drive-in?" Rourke asked.

"Very simple, really, we threatened Fulsom with killing you. He obliged by telling us. He felt obligated. We now have all of your men."

"Hell," Rourke said, his voice low, "they aren't my men."

"Whoever they are, if you cooperate, they will go

free. If you don't, they will be executed. And if they are freed, of course, their weapons will not be returned as yours have been. Come, I have a woman you might like to meet. Don't worry."

"I won't," Rourke said, slinging the CAR-15 from his right shoulder, hooking his right thumb in the carry handle.

"Good," Korcinski said and smiled.

Rourke followed the Soviet colonel out of the clearing and down a rough dirt path into the deeper part of the woods. He resettled the binoculars and the musette bag on his left shoulder as he walked, uncertain what Korcinski planned.

In another, smaller clearing, a staff car waited, its headlights burning and drawing swarms of night flies and moths. In the edge of the light beams stood a woman, slender, wearing a Soviet uniform, the skirt seemingly too long, Rourke observed.

Korcinski walked toward her, Rourke beside him. Korcinski stopped, saying, "This young woman has a personal message for you, Mr. Rourke."

As Korcinski started to turn away, Rourke looked at him, whispering, "What's to stop me from killing both of you?"

Korcinski, half-turned away, looked at Rourke across his left shoulder, "You are not a murderer or an assassin—and, were you to do such a rash thing, or attempt to take one or the other of us hostage, all your men—or whose men they are—would be executed."

"I'm not a murderer, but you are?"

"Something like that, if you chose to think of it that way," Korcinski said, turning the rest of the way around and walking away.

Rourke looked at the woman. She was tall and young, as he had thought. "Who are—"

"I am instructed to tell you only this. I am General Ishmael Varakov's personal secretary. He asked that I give you this note, then you return the note to me after you have read it."

Rourke took the square envelope, broke the red wax seal on the flap, removed and unfolded the note. He bent toward the light from the headlights to read it: "Rourke—You have impressed me with your singular competence and daring. The contents of this note are to be held in the strictest confidence. I will assume that I have your word as a gentleman on that. And it is an affair of gentlemen I discuss here. My niece, Natalia, the wife of Vladmir Karamatsov, is quite fond of you, and I understand though nothing actually transpired between you, that you both became close as friends. Her husband has quite recently beaten her severely, almost killing her toward the end, compelling her to defend herself. She is a faithful wife in her fashion, and would likely return to Karamatsov sooner or later. I fear, as her uncle, that Karamatsov will attack her again, this time permanently injuring her or perhaps killing her. Because of political problems, I cannot kill Karamatsov with my bare hands as I would like.

"I ask that you do this for me, however you wish—I have enclosed his projected itinerary for tomorrow. If you do this thing, all your comrades will be freed, the head of the American KGB will have been liquidated—surely something you can count as a benefit—and, more important to both of us, Natalia's future safety will be secured. I ask this as one man of honor to another—despite our political differences. I will not consider myself indebted to you for this other than personally.

"Karamatsov is a madman and for all our sakes must be destroyed."

The letter was signed with a large letter V.

Rourke folded the letter, then handed it back to the woman, squinting at her eyes in the harsh illumination of the headlights.

She asked in the good enough English, "I am instructed to ask you for a yes or no answer."

"Why me?"

"I know nothing about the letter. The General speaks excellent English and wrote it personally."

"Yes," Rourke said slowly.

"Here," she said, handing Rourke a small envelope. He opened it: it was an agenda for the next day, detailing Karamatsov's movements.

"All right," Rourke said. He folded the paper again, and placed it in the breast pocket of his shirt. "Anything else?"

"The General said if you said 'yes' I was to say, 'good luck'."

Rourke looked at her a moment. "You're wearing your skirt too long. And thanks for the good wishes."

Chapter 36

Vladmir Karamatsov opened his eyes and looked through the motel balcony door—the motel was now the transient and bachelor officers quarters. It was light, but rising from the bed and going toward the floor to ceiling glass, he opened the curtains wider and saw the fog. He slipped the window open to his left and smelled at it: the fog seemed rank and foul and was cool—cold almost.

He closed the window, leaving the top-floor drapes open, staring in the gray light at the woman on the bed. She was moving slightly, turning into the covers, cold apparently.

He stared at her, walking across the room. He didn't exactly know why, but he had slapped her several times; there was a bruise on her left cheek as she rolled toward the window, then back away from it. Unlike Natalia, she had liked the brutality. It was a side of himself to which he was yet unaccustomed;

he liked the brutality almost more than the sex afterward.

Karamatsov walked into the bathroom, urinated, then looked at his face in the mirror. There were still bruises from where Natalia had struck him when she had so suddenly decided to defend herself. He walked back into the bedroom and looked at the blond-haired woman sleeping there. He wondered, almost absently, what it would be like to kill Natalia. He shook his head to clear the thought away.

Returning to the bathroom, he lathered his face and began to shave. He had picked up the Hoffritz razor at an exclusive shop in Rio. His face hurt where the bruises were as he grimaced in order to smooth the skin to shave closer. He made a mental note to inquire about the noise of explosions that previous morning. He had been out of the city, interrogating some of the former university personnel at the detention center, trying to learn the whereabouts of the former astronaut, Jim Colfax. He had thought, too, that faintly in the distance the previous night he had heard gunfire. There was a time he would have run to the sound, he thought. But he had been busy, playing the games with the woman on the bed, making her feel pain, which she seemed so to delight in.

He brushed his teeth, carefully visually inspecting them in the bathroom mirror, the four stainless-steel teeth that made a permanent bridge in the lower right side of his mouth. They were new and still uncomfortable. Before the war, when his primary duties had been to pose as anyone but a Russian, he would never have allowed the stainless-steel teeth—only Soviet dentists used them. Buttons stitched in a cross shape showed you had a European tailor, keeping your fork in your left hand when you ate showed you were not American. There had been so many little things under which to submerge one's own personality, Karamatsov thought.

He started the water in the shower; he liked American plumbing. He washed his body, washed his hair, then rinsed under cold water for several minutes, thinking. After stepping out of the water and toweling himself dry, he began to dress. Civilian clothes again today, he thought: American blue jeans and a knit shirt, dark blue. He slipped on the shoulder holster for the Smith & Wesson Model 59. Since Natalia had taken his little revolver he had found a replacement, slipping that into its belt holster and sliding the holster in place. He liked the revolver best, but the double-column 9mm Model 59 had firepower, and that was sometimes needed.

He pulled a lined windbreaker from the closet and slipped it over the shirt and shoulder holster, then a baseball cap that read "Cat" on the front and advertised some sort of tractor. There was still the desire to look like the enemy, he thought, smiling at his American image in the mirror.

He looked at the woman on the bed, decided not to wake her; she would likely come back again tonight. After it became known she had slept with one of the Russian conquerors, she would likely have no place else to go.

He walked downstairs to the restaurant, now run by orderlies from the officers' mess. American food was served because it was easier to obtain—he

197

ordered steak and eggs with hash browned potatoes. They served grits; he didn't like grits because they stuck sometimes in the new stainless-steel bridgework. Americans were forced to work in the kitchen, too, and grits would be too easy in which to disguise ground glass.

He had his third cup of coffee, determined mentally his order of work and pulled the baseball cap back in place. The fog had not dissipated; he had watched through the window. A few cars moved slowly on the street, those with travel and gasoline permits. Several people, shoulders hunched, eyes down, walked along the sidewalks. There was no work, no food, nowhere to go for these Americans. He decided to recommend to Varakov that the unproductive persons—those over age, those infirm, etc.—be liquidated in order that they be less of a burden for the new order. He doubted though that the soft-hearted Varakov would go along with the idea.

Varakov, he thought. He stopped on the steps and lit a cigarette, looking across the street. That was his next project: eliminate Varakov and assume his command. He—Karamatsov—would show the Politburo, the Premier, all of them, how a conquered nation could be subdued, whipped into line, then made productive once again. The very next project, he thought, after arranging something nice for Natalia. Perhaps, he thought, reconsidering, he could use Natalia to destroy her uncle—eliminate them both. He had no use for a wife who had no use for him. There were many women like the blonde, ones who didn't think they were angels or precious flowers—ones who would make a man feel like a god.

He started toward the sidewalk, walking each morning since he had arrived to military headquarters. Exercise was good for a man.

Chapter 37

Rourke had driven through the night, returned to the retreat by the most circuitous route to determine he wasn't followed. He had showered, changed, eaten, had a drink and discussed what he had to do with Paul Rubenstein. While Rourke had cleaned and checked his weapons, they had discussed the letter from Varakov and Rourke's promise to Natalia not to kill her husband. He disliked being cast in the role of an assassin.

Yet, if Karamatsov didn't die, and if Karamatsov found out about the plan, he would most assuredly blame his wife and try to get his revenge. Perhaps, too, Rourke had thought out loud, Karamatsov would kill her anyway. He had gotten the impression when they had met in Texas that, aside from total ruthlessness, Karamatsov was also more than slightly insane.

And now, having ridden through the fog through

the early-morning hours, a fresh bandage in place on his cheek where he had skinned it, his guns freshly cleaned and checked and loaded, his knives touched up on the whetstone, he knew what he would do.

He dismounted the bike, seeing Karamatsov coming down the steps and onto the sidewalk and starting his way. Rourke stripped off his leather jacket and the pistol belt with the Government .45.

He had already cocked and locked the twin Detonics stainless pistols, and they rode now in their shoulder holsters under his armpits. The harness made in a rough figure eight across his shoulders and back over the light-blue shirt, he stepped from the alley into the foggy street, rolling his sleeves up as he walked. Karamatsov had not seen him yet. He trusted to Varakov that Soviet patrols would be conspicuously absent.

Rourke stopped, taking one of the small cigars from his shirt pocket, lighting it in the blue-yellow flame of the battered Zippo lighter. He dropped the lighter in the pocket of his Levi's, his combat boots clicking with hollow sounds on the pavement.

He stripped the sunglasses from his face and pocketed them, the glare of the fog making him change his mind and put them back on. He stopped in the middle of the street, then walked to the curb and onto the sidewalk.

He stopped again, two thin streams of gray smoke issuing from his nostrils as he exhaled. Karamatsov had finally seen him.

Chapter 38

Paul Rubenstein squatted on his haunches on the roof line of what had once been a restaurant, the Steyr-Mannlicher SSG in his hands, the 3 x 9 scope set to six power for the distance, a round chambered in the synthetic stocked Parkerized bolt action.

Rourke had anticipated that Varakov would perhaps have Karamatsov dogged by a sniper, to kill Rourke after he killed Karamatsov. Paul smiled, thinking that for once John Rourke had been wrong. He stopped smiling as he saw Rourke stop in the street, the distance separating Rourke from Karamatsov less than twenty-five yards. It was a gunfight—it was insanity, Rubenstein thought. He wished he could hear the words. He watched as both men looked from side to side to make sure, Rubenstein guessed, that no innocent bystanders were in the line of fire. He wished also that Rourke would have let him do it, just snap the trigger and let

Karamatsov fall. He shifted the scope slightly and framed the crosshairs on Karamatsov's head; it would be so easy.

His hands sweated—it wouldn't be easy at all, he thought. And that wasn't Rourke's way of things. It always had to be fair. "Damn," the young, slightly balding man muttered, his glasses steaming over his own perspiration. The perspiration was from fear that perhaps Rourke wasn't invincible as he had always seemed to be ever since they had met after the plane crash in New Mexico on the night of the war.

"Damn," he whispered to himself, quickly scanning again for snipers, then focusing on Rourke, then Karamatsov, then cutting the power so he could see both men as they faced each other.

Chapter 39

Rourke almost whispered, "Right here okay?"

"For what, Rourke, are you going to tell me how wonderful my wife was in bed?"

"We never saw a bed. I told you before, nothing happened."

"Then why here, why now. Why?"

"A long story," Rourke observed. "Go for your gun whenever you want—if you like, I'll wait while you ditch your coat."

"All right," Karamatsov snapped, stripping the coat from his shoulders, throwing it down on the sidewalk, pulling the baseball cap low over his eyes. "One gun, two. I have never been in a Western gunfight before."

"I don't think you will be again. It's not technique that counts, not so much. It's not just speed. It's accuracy. That's why I figured twenty-five yards—makes it more even for you against me. I

204

might be faster, but you're probably just as accurate."

"I'm so touched, Rourke. I can see why Natalia thinks so highly of you. And you can have her—the slut. The moment my back was turned, after all my years of fidelity to her—even now I am still faithful to her. And she, you—you plot to murder me."

"If it matters," Rourke said softly, his eyes riveted to Karamatsov's eyes. "She doesn't know a thing about this. I even promised her once I wouldn't kill you. If I ever meet her again, she'll probably hate me for killing you."

"You mean, if you kill me," Karamatsov snapped, his voice sounding higher-pitched, the words clipped and nasal.

"Have it your way—if. Then—whenever you're ready—just go for it. I'll watch your eyes, and I'll know when to make my move."

"Idiot! American fool!"

"I'll admit two grown men standing in the street and shooting at each other isn't too smart. It was just the fairest thing I could come up with on the spur of the moment," Rourke said, rolling the cigar in the left corner of his mouth, clenching his teeth.

"Doesn't someone drop a handkerchief?"

"That's only in movies," Rourke answered.

Karamatsov edged, sidestepping slowly to his left, off the curb and into the street.

Rourke edged left as well, his eyes watching Karamatsov's eyes, the fog starting to lift and swirl as the wind picked up, sunlight breaking through. Rourke squinted, despite the glasses, against the glare of the sun on the gray fog.

It was misleading, he thought, to say you watched the eyes. Karamatsov had probably assumed as much. At twenty-five yards or so, the eyes themselves would be hard or impossible to see clearly. You watched instead the set of the eyes, he thought, the almost imperceptible tightening of the muscles around them, the little squint that—

Rourke saw the eyes set.

Karamatsov's right hand flashed up toward the Model 59 in the shoulder rig, the thumbsnap breaking with an almost audible click, the gun's muzzle straightening out as Karamatsov took a half-step right and crouched, his left hand moving to help grasp the gun, the hat caught up by a gust of wind and sailing from his head.

Rourke's right hand moved first, then his left, the right hand bringing the first Detonics on line, the safety swept off under his thumb as the gun had cleared the leather, the gun in the left hand moving on line as Rourke triggered the first shot.

Rourke saw the flash against the fog of Karamatsov's pistol, the stainless Detonics bucking through recoil in Rourke's right hand, then the left gun firing, then the right and the left simultaneously.

Karamatsov flew up off the ground almost a foot, Rourke judged, the gun in Karamatsov's hands firing up into the air—a second round. The Russian's body twitched in midair, then twitched and lurched twice more as it fell, the Russian's gun firing again into the street. A window smashed on the other side. His body rolled over face down, the right arm and left leg twitching, shivering, then stopping. There was no more movement.

Rourke thumbed up the safety on the pistol in his right hand and jabbed it into his belt, shifted the gun in his left hand to his right, thumbed up the safety and held the gun limp at his side against his thigh, walking forward, slowly, then stopping and rolling over the Russian's body with his combat-booted foot, his right thumb poised over the safety of his pistol.

There were four dark-red patches on Karamatsov's trunk.

Rourke bent over and, with the thumb of his left hand, closed the eyelids.

"Done," he whispered.

Chapter 40

The chill wind lashed at John Rourke's face and hair as he bent low over the Harley-Davidson. The engine throbbed between his thighs, the sound of it combined with the wind roaring in his ears. He glanced to his right, Rubenstein beside and slightly behind him.

The escape from town had been surprisingly easy. Rourke decided Varakov was indeed a man of his word, but there was no way Rourke could imagine Korcinski keeping to his portion of the bargain and releasing the rest of the men from the Resistance. He could simply leave it out of his report to Varakov that they had been executed, but he would have waited for something to happen, some reason for Rourke's release and once news of the death of Karamatsov reached him, Korcinski would know—it would all be clear. They would all be dead.

Rourke turned and glanced toward Rubenstein,

trying to hear what the younger man was shouting over the slipstream and vibration of the engines. "Where—are—we—going?"

Rourke smiled, his lips curled back against the pressure of the wind, the speedometer on the bike over seventy. "To a reunion," he shouted, then seeing the puzzled look on Paul Rubenstein's face, he repeated, only shouting louder, more slowly, "To—a—re—union!"

Rourke turned and bent over the bike again. The fog was all but lifted and it was nearly nine A.M. as he glanced at the black face of the Rolex Oyster Perpetual Submariner on his left wrist—executions, he thought, were usually an early morning affair. "Hurry," he shouted to his side toward Rubenstein, then gave the bike more throttle.

Rourke slowed the Harley dramatically, making his turn wide onto the gravel road, taking him off the main highway and into the woods and down toward the clearing far beyond where he determined the hostage Resistance fighters were still being kept. He had judged Korcinski as being competent yet vain. He would never expect Rourke to come back and try to rescue his "comrades."

Rourke counted heavily on that, for even with Paul Rubenstein at his side the odds were heavily stacked against him.

Rourke slowed his jet-black Harley even more, curving into a gentle arc and stopping. Rubenstein passed him, then cut back, and stopped beside him, facing him.

"Where, John?"

"Up there—maybe two miles through the

woods—too many Russians on the highways,"
Rourke rasped back, winded.

"We got a chance?"

Rourke smiled. "If we didn't have a chance we
wouldn't be here."

Rourke started the Harley again, slower this time
because of the roughness of the dirt road he
followed.

Rourke reviewed the details of his plan, the only
way he thought he had a chance. If nothing were
transpiring as he reached the clearing he would wait,
wait for the Resistance fighters to be led from
wherever they were being held to a spot where they
would be shot. He remembered the Soviet massacre
of the Polish officer corps during World War
II—the Katyn Forest Massacre. They had used German weapons and tried to blame the Germans for
the mass murder. Some clever investigator had
discovered the real truth, examining the rope with
which the victims had been bound—they were Russian made. Perhaps Korcinski would try to arrange
things so that it appeared the Resistance people had
fought among themselves and use the captured
weapons from the fighters to execute them.

Rourke drove his bike as quickly as he dared
through the woods, glancing every few minutes at
the Rolex, watching the seconds tick away, wondering if the hostages were still alive.

After several more minutes, Rourke slowed his
bike, signaling with one hand for Rubenstein—behind him—to do the same. Stopping,
Rourke glanced back across his right shoulder.
"Over there, maybe five hundred yards. Come on."

Rourke dismounted, hauling his bike into the trees, taking the bayonet from his belt, and hacking away at the brush to camouflage it. Rubenstein did the same a few yards from him.

"You want the SSG?" Rubenstein asked. Rourke shook his head no, unslinging the CAR-15 from his back and working the ears on the bolt, chambering a round, then slipping the safety on. The rifle, stock collapsed, slung under his right shoulder, his fist wrapped around the pistol grip, he started forward, Rubenstein moving behind him as Rourke glanced back.

The air was cold, damp, and foul-smelling from the patches of fog still clinging in the shadows of the trees low along the ground. Rourke walked slightly stooped over, threading his way under low branches around bushes laden with two-inch-long thorns, bright-green-leaved brush swatting at his hands and thighs as he pushed his way past.

Judging he'd gone half the distance, he signaled a stop with his left hand, held a finger to his lips for silence and drooping into a low crouch, moved ahead. After what Rourke judged as another fifty yards, he stopped again, hearing the faint sound of voices. He moved laterally, trying to line up the sound of the voices with the approximate position of the clearing, stopped, hearing the voices more clearly, but still unable to tell the words, then started forward again.

He moved what he judged as slightly more than a hundred yards, stopped, and listened. There were orders being shouted. He thought he faintly recognized Korcinski's voice. Dropping to the ground, Rourke signaled Rubenstein to do the same. Both men moved ahead on their knees and elbows, crawling over the rough ground, cautious to avoid snapping a dried twig or some other casual noise that might betray them.

Again Rourke signaled a stop, seeing the outline of the upper half of a uniformed man above a low-rising natural hedgerow. Rourke motioned Rubenstein to stay back, handing him off the CAR-15 and palming out the Sting IA from inside his trousers, then on knees and elbows he inched forward.

Again Rourke stopped, the sentry clearly in view, an AK-47 at high port as the man stared over the hedgerow, Rourke beneath his line of sight. There was no chance of getting around behind the man, Rourke decided, pushing himself up slightly and scanning the woods as best he could for signs of other sentries. He picked one man on the far side of the clearing, opposite this man and turned back to the clearing, so far staying away from Rourke's own position. Then Rourke spotted a third man, far to his left, standing beside the collection of Soviet vehicles. Korcinski's staff car was there, Rourke doubted the man had spent the night in the open field in the woods. Perhaps he had returned to preside over the execution. There were more orders barked from the clearing, and now Rourke recognized Korcinski's voice, in Russian, the colonel ordering the hostages be brought from the trucks where they were being held. Rourke spotted the fourth sentry far to his right by two large tents, these apparently set up to house the men who had guarded the hostages over night.

There was activity in the clearing, men grumbling in Russian as soldiers grumble in any tongue, the sounds of rifle actions being checked. The execution, Rourke realized, was imminent. He looked back to the sentry almost immediately ahead of him, still staring out blankly over the hedgerow.

Rourke edged forward, the Sting clamped in his teeth. It was risky, what he planned, but it was all he could do.

He was less than five feet from the sentry now, slightly to the soldier's right.

Rourke got his knees up under him in a crouch, then scanning from right to left to see if he were being watched, he pushed himself to his feet, reaching out with his left hand, the arm extended fully, snatching his fist toward the right side of the Russian soldier's face, his right arm lunging forward like a fencer, the black chrome Sting clenched in his right fist, his thumb braced against the grooved steel handle portion of the knife, the spear point tip of the blade punching in hard in the hollow behind the chin to cut the vocal chords and stifle any cry. The Russian's eyes were wide with pain and horror as Rourke withdrew the knife, then raked it left to right across the man's already bleeding throat, catching the soldier as he fell forward toward him, already dead, the look of puzzlement still in the eyes.

Rourke eased the body to the ground, wiping the blood from his hands on the soldier's uniform shirt.

Rourke dragged the body under a bush, then stripped away the ammo from the man's belt, and snatched up the AK-47, looking behind him, signaling Rubenstein to come ahead.

Rourke inched into the hedgerow, a full view now of the clearing showed perhaps a dozen Russian soldiers being formed up into a long single rank. The corners of Rourke's mouth turned down as he squinted at the weapons the men held—the motley collection used by the Resistance people and Reed and his men.

Rourke looked to his left and saw Reed, the corporal, the other two men, Fulsom, and Darren Ball, and the twenty or so others who had survived the previous night's fiasco being marched from the trucks parked at the far end of the clearing toward the center of the clearing. A tall stand of pines made a salient into the clearing.

The execution, Rourke realized.

Suddenly, Rubenstein was beside him. He started to speak and Rourke held up a finger to his lips, signaling silence and nodding to Paul that he too saw the preparations for the mass murder.

Rourke took back his CAR-15, passed over the spare magazines for the AK-47, then the gun itself to Rubenstein, pointing out to him the safety selector. Busily, Rubenstein stuffed the spare magazines into the belt cinched around his waist, nodding.

Rourke gestured to Rubenstein, then pointed out into the clearing toward where the firing squad was formed. The Resistance people were already straggling toward it. He pointed toward his own mouth and opened it wide as though shouting, pointed to the AK-47 in Rubenstein's hands, then held his own hands, as if holding some kind of invisible submachine gun, then swept the imaginary weapon from side to side, then pointed back at the ranked firing squad. Rubenstein nodded grimly.

Rourke signaled with his fingers, a walking motion to Rubenstein and then pointed along the tree line. Again, the younger man nodded. Rourke snatched up the CAR-15 and removed the scope covers, then pushed himself up into a crouch and started off to the right, toward the stand of pines serving as the backstop for the firing squad's bullets.

Rourke reached the trees, flattening himself behind one as best he could, glancing down to his weapon, slowly, as noislessly as possible, telescoping the collapsible stock, entwining his left arm in the sling—a hasty sling—looking right and left, then edging forward.

The Resistance fighters and Reed and his men partially shielded Rourke, he realized, from the view of the firing squad as he raced in a low crouch toward the center of the stand.

Rourke could hear the commands to the firing squad: "Ready!"

Rourke heard the actions of the strange assortment of weapons being worked, through the trees in the clearing beyond he could see the Russian guards who had escorted the hostages drawing back. He could see Korcinski, the greatcoat open, the swagger stick braced in his gloved hands, then slowly raising in his right hand.

"Aim!" another officer's voice shouted.

Rourke could see the swagger stick at full elevation, watched the muscles on Korcinski's face tense as Rourke settled the crosshairs beyond the face at the hand holding the swagger stick.

Rourke, on one knee in the densest portion of the

stand of pines, shouted, "Reed, Fulsom, Ball—hit the dirt!" He fired, his first slug kicking at the swagger stick in Korcinski's gloved right hand, Korcinski falling back. Rourke swept the scope to Korcinski's head, Rubenstein's gunfire with the AK-47 already mowing into the line of executioners, some of the men running and throwing down the unfamiliar weapons they held, some starting to shoot back.

Rourke fired the CAR-15 again, this time the 5.56mm solid punching in at the peak of Korcinski's hat, the hat blowing off Korcinski's head. Rourke shouted, "Next one kills you—call a ceasefire!"

He watched Korcinski's head through the glass of the scope, bullets whizzing into trees around him, then above the clatter of gunfire Rourke heard Korcinski shout, watching the lips move through the scope; "Cease fire! Immediately! Cease fire!"

The gunfire slowly waned, Rourke, the rifle shouldered, rising to his feet, Korcinski's head still under his crosshairs.

Rourke shouted, "Reed, you and the rest of the men get your weapons and gear. Disarm the Russians—move it!"

At the back of his mind Rourke realized the gunfire might bring more of the Soviet troops down on him, or perhaps one of the Russians out there would take it into his head to become a hero and snatch up a gun and start shooting. "Hurry!" Rourke shouted hoarsely, moving slowly through the trees toward Korcinski, the scope never leaving Korcinski's head. "Korcinski," Rourke rasped, then in Russian said, "Tell your men that if there are any thoughts of heroics to forget them—you will be the first to die—I promise. A bullet right in the head."

Korcinski, his jaw dropping, shouted to his men, "Do as he says!"

Rourke stopped walking, ten feet from the Russian, slowly lowering the rifle, collapsing the stock, holding it dead level on Korcinski.

He heard Reed's voice, "All right—line 'em all up so we can get out of here."

"Kill 'em," Darren Ball shouted.

Rourke glanced to his left briefly, saw Ball raising an AR-15 toward the face of a Soviet lieutenant.

"Move and you're dead," Rourke snapped to Korcinski, then wheeled to his left, snapping off two quick shots with the CAR-15 splintering the black synthetic buttstock of the rifle, Ball spinning toward him.

Rourke shifted the CAR-15 to his left hand, snatching the Metalifed Government Model Colt from the hip holster and jerking back the hammer, the gun aimed at Korcinski's midsection. Rourke's eyes darted back and forth between the two men.

"What the hell you do that for?" Ball snapped.

"You were going to execute that man," Rourke said, his voice low.

"So, what the hell?"

"So," Rourke answered slowly, "murder isn't any better if you're doing it, or they're doing it. Touch a gun to anyone and I'll drop you—I swear it."

"Mr. Good Guy, huh? Bullshit!"

Rourke stared at Ball's eyes. "You've got a pistol in your belt; try using it."

Ball's right hand edged half way to his belt line, the shattered buttstock of the rifle in pieces at his feet. "Try using it," Rourke repeated. If he and Ball were to have it out, Rourke wanted it now.

"No," Ball rasped. "No, I heard why they let you go, what you did to Karamatsov—no, not now, not ever."

Rourke turned his attention back toward Korcinski, the Russian, in English, saying, "Strange behavior for Varåkov's private assassin. Karamatsov was—what is the word?—a bastard, I think."

"More or less," Rourke commented, his voice low. "You're no prince yourself, though."

Then, turning and shouting over his shoulder, Rourke said, "All of you—split up in small groups, take off through the woods. Reed, you and your men stick with me. Fulsom too." Then turning to Ball, Rourke told the one-legged man, "Darren, steal a vehicle, take about five or six men with you. Torch it under some bridge when you're ready to get rid of it."

" 'Til we meet again," the ex-mercenary smiled.

" 'Til we meet again," Rourke echoed, Ball already starting to limp away.

As the Resistance fighters began to disperse, Rourke had Rubenstein take over watching Korcinski, then helped Reed and his men and Fulsom load every Soviet weapon they could find aboard a truck. As they loaded the last machine gun aboard the truck, Rourke turned to Fulsom, "At least you've got some of the weapons you needed."

"Was there a traitor with us?"

"No, higher up I think." Looking at Reed, Rourke continued, "Captain Reed's men kept radioing what we were doing—I think it's somebody back in Texas."

"No way, Rourke, that's out of line—I call in directly to command headquarters. Only the top people know—"

"Then it must be one of the top people," Rourke said matter-of-factly. "There was evidence of that when they so neatly snatched Chambers at the airfield, where he'd landed in Texas."

"You mean Karamatsov had somebody when he gunned down that pilot?"

"Yeah," Rourke rasped, "and to nail us last night, Varakov must have him now. There's one sure way to know—only one." Rourke turned to Fulsom. "Where's Jim Colfax supposed to be?"

"Up in the mountains near Helen, Georgia—got a Swiss chalet-like house up there he inherited when his brother died. One of my guys spotted him still at the house two days ago. My man had seen him on TV."

"Where exactly," Rourke said.

"I'll draw you out a map, and thanks, Rourke. We'll look for your family. How do we contact you?"

"You contact Army Intelligence, I'll contact them," Rourke told Fulsom.

"What about the traitor?" Reed asked.

"We'll know for sure there is one at your headquarters after today. Helen's about two hours from here. I used to take Sarah and the kids there. Beautiful place. You have your man radio in just like he normally would. Tell them you expect to be up there in three hours. The Russians won't pass up a chance to get Colfax and us all at the same time so they'll wait, but we'll be there an hour earlier."

"Is that enough time?" Reed asked.

"I'm leaving now with Paul. The bikes can make better time. Have Fulsom give you another map like the one he's making for me, then you follow in one of the Russian vehicles. Have Fulsom show you some side roads and possible alternates on your own maps. And we'll rendezvous at Colfax's place. Leave two of your men some distance off to warn us when the Russians begin to show."

"Rourke?"

"Yeah?"

"Forget about that fight, huh? I owe you my neck."

"What fight?" Rourke smiled, turning away and starting back toward Rubenstein, buttonholing Reed's corporal to keep the drop on Korcinski after Rourke and Rubenstein left.

Chapter 41

Rourke ran through the woods, Paul Rubenstein beside and slightly behind him, both men stopping where they'd left the bikes camouflaged behind brush, stripping the brush away and mounting up.

"We're going back up into the mountains?"

"Yeah, after the astronaut, Colfax. Should have the Russians right behind us—probably use helicopters to get up there—might be a lot of shooting," Rourke added, looking at the younger man.

"So, I should be used to it by now?" Rubenstein laughed and Rourke slapped him on the shoulder, then looked at him. "What are you looking at me like that for?"

"You're a good friend, Paul," Rourke said quietly, turned away, and mounted his Harley.

It began to mist less than ten minutes into the two-hour ride into the mountains, and soon the mist turned into a driving, road-slicking rain. Rourke, with Rubenstein riding dead even beside him to minimize the spray of the wheels against the highway, was soaked through.

Because of the driving rain, their speed was cut just to keep control, and, as Rourke turned off the highway onto the side road Fulsom had indicated for him, he glanced at his watch. It had taken slightly over two and one-half hours and might well take Reed, unfamiliar with the area, even longer.

Rourke pulled in at the side of the single-lane, black-topped access road, turned to Paul Rubenstein as he pushed his fingers through his soaking wet hair, his eyes half closed against the downpour. "The Colfax place should be at the end of this road, then a driveway. There's a wooded area behind the house. No suitable spot for the helicopters to land if the Soviets use Air Cavalry, but they might be able to rapel down to the ground. They're going to want Colfax alive to get the information on the Eden Project—the same as we want. Come on."

Rubenstein nodded, wet, looking disgusted, his glasses pocketed and his deep set eyes squinted, but unlike Rourke's not just against the rain. Rubenstein, Rourke knew, needed the glasses to see properly.

Rourke started up the single-lane road, traveling slowly, Rubenstein behind him. The blacktop was slick and the ditches along both sides of the road were running to overflowing in the heavy rain, the water there a washed-out blood red from the clay.

At the end of the road was a graveled driveway and Rourke cut left, turning onto it, exhaling hard in relief at the more stable road surface, the bike crunching over the wet, white gravel chunks, a house looking as though it had been lifted from the Bavarian Alps directly ahead.

The cuckoo-clocklike structure had a second-floor porch traveling the width of the house, shuttered windows and doorways facing onto it, below a smaller porch, ornamental, gingerbread style woodwork, brightly painted, adorning each cornice and corner.

Rourke stopped his bike ten feet from the house, kicked out the stand, and dismounted. The CAR-15—the muzzle cap in place and dust cover closed—slung muzzle down across his back, his up-turned collar streaming water into his shirt. He pushed his wet hair from his forehead and walked toward the small first-floor porch, looking up at the second floor for some sign of habitation. The gravel crunched beside him and Rourke glanced to his right. Paul Rubenstein was beside him.

"Paul—go around back—I don't want Colfax to duck out on us."

The younger man nodded, his thinning hair plastered to his forehead by the rain, then disappeared to Rourke's left around the side of the house. Rourke stepped onto the porch, the drumming of the rain on the porch above him intense, the sound of rushing water through the downspouts from the roof-line gutters like a torrent.

He fished into his wallet, pulled the plastic coated CIA identity card from it, then replaced the wallet in his pocket. He searched the door for a bell, found none and hammered on the fake Dutch door with his left fist. "My name is Rourke," he shouted. "I'm with American Intelligence—CIA card here in my hand," and he turned the card toward the curtained windows in case Colfax were looking through a slit.

"Jim Colfax—I'm here to help you," Rourke shouted.

Then there was another shout, Paul Rubenstein, the voice clear over the drumming of the rain, the words though hard to make out.

Rourke glanced from side to side, pocketed the CIA card, and flipped the porch railing, his boots splattering down into the mud beside the porch, almost losing his footing as he ran around the side of the house.

Rubenstein was pointing into the tall, widely spaced stand of pines in the backlot. "Colfax, a white-haired guy with a crewcut?"

"Yeah—I think so," Rourke shouted back over the rain.

"He's out there," Rubenstein said, breathless sounding. "I saw him—must have heard us coming up and took off. You said he has heart trouble, that's why he quit the astronaut program?"

"Yeah," Rourke answered.

"Then we'd better hurry and stop him. I'm not sure, but either he's got a funny way of running or he was holding both hands over his chest."

"My God!" Rourke shouted, already breaking into a dead run for the trees, "Get your bike and come on," Rourke snapped over his shoulder. Rourke hit the tree line, his right hand curling around one of the narrow pine trunks, stopping, swinging around the trunk, scanning the woods right and left. He spotted movement, then saw a white-haired man running up the steeply sloping grade a hundred yards deeper into the pines.

"Colfax!" he shouted over the drumming of the rain. "Colfax! Jim Colfax. I'm an American. I don't want to hurt you. I'm here to help." The man started running.

Shaking his head, Rourke glanced behind him for Rubenstein and the bike, saw him coming and yelled, "'Over here—toward the slope, Paul," then started running through the trees, dodging the sparse brush, jumping deadfalls, his feet slipping in the mud, catching himself on his hands, pushing to his feet and continuing to run. Rourke could see Colfax up ahead, see Rubenstein zig-zagging through the trees trying to cut Colfax off. "Colfax! Wait, man!" Rourke shouted, stopping, scanning the trees ahead, spotting the white hair, then starting to run again.

Rourke missed a deadfall, half stumbled, and caught himself, slithering across the mud, then getting half to his feet. Rubenstein was at the far edge of the woods, and Colfax was running laterally to Rourke's left along the slope.

Shaking his head, Rourke picked himself up and started running. "Colfax—wait!"

Colfax turned, started running again and, as Rourke started to shout once more, Rourke could see the white-haired, athletic man stumble and fall, rolling down the slope, his body slithering across the red mud of clay wash and colliding against a tree stump and stopping.

"Over here!" Rourke shouted to Rubenstein, waving his left arm as he ran toward Colfax.

Rourke dropped to his knees in the mud, lifting Colfax's face to feel for a pulse.

There was none. "The Eden Project," Rourke whispered. The white-haired man's eyelids rolled open as the head sank from Rourke's hands.

"Can't you do anything?"

Rourke looked up at the face belonging to the voice. "No, Paul—if I had a hospital or a trained cardiac team—maybe I could start the heart again. He was dead before I reached him. The eyelids just came open as a reflex action when I bent his head away. He's gone."

"Then what's up there—what's the Eden Project, John?"

Rourke set the white-haired man's head down on the ground, closing the eyelids with his thumbs, then stood and stared up at the gray sky, rain washing across his face.

He clapped Rubenstein on the shoulder, starting back toward Rubenstein's bike. "The Russians'll bury him." Then, "What's up there, hmmm? Cheer up, Paul, maybe it isn't a doomsday machine or a weapon of some sort. Who knows—maybe the Eden Project is something that'll do some good. Maybe." Rourke almost repeated "who knows" but a wry smile crossed his lips. The last man who knew was dead.

Chapter 42

The Russians came, ransacking the house, searching the woods. Rourke and Rubenstein had completed searching the house long before Reed had arrived, gone with Reed to a place of concealment on high ground in a cleft of rocks long before the Soviet helicopter's whirring had filled the air and drowned out the rain.

"I guess I can tell you," Reed said.

Rourke looked at him, then hunched back more into the rock, not bothering to watch the Russians anymore. He lighted one of his cigars, trying to shake the dampness in his clothing and in his bones. "Tell me what?"

"Well—before I do—Fulsom. We used my radio. He wanted to do something for you. He's got a contact in the Resistance up in Tennessee. Hadn't said anything to you because he didn't want to get any false hopes up. Got a message out last night before

227

the raid and the Resistance man in Tennessee promised he'd check around. Fulsom just had a feeling about it. Made me call in on their frequency. Well, guy owns a farm, his wife is the aunt of the only survivor of the Jenkins family you mentioned. The guy was a retired Army sergeant. His son, anyway, just joined up with him, got wounded last night. They talked. Sarah and your kids are up at his farm—been there the last few days."

Rourke pushed away from the rocks. The cigar fell from his mouth, burning at his trousers as he brushed it away. "Where," Rourke said, grasping Reed's collar.

"Here." Reed handed Rourke a dirty, folded Tennessee highway map. "It's marked—up near some place called Mt. Eagle in the mountains. You know it."

"What," Rourke said absently, not even opening the map, just staring at it in his hands. "Yeah, Mt. Eagle, yeah, I know it."

"John, thank God."

Rubenstein threw his arms around Rourke, and Rourke slapped the younger man on the back.

"Reed," Rourke stammered. "Fulsom—can you thank him for me, will you—?"

"I'll see him. Just in case, I'm leaving Paul the radio set we have and some spare parts from the kit. You want to contact us, the frequency'll be marked. One other thing."

"Yeah," Rourke said, already standing at the edge of the rocks and staring down at the departing Russian troops. There was a small residual team up in the woods, carrying out the rubber bagged body of Colfax. "Looks like they're going to give him a decent burial anyway."

"John, they'll think maybe you found out before Colfax died. The Russians'll want you. They want to know what the Eden Project was—almost more than we do. And you were right about that traitor—looks there's someone in Chambers's advisors who works for the Communists."

Almost disinterested, Rourke stuck out his hand. Reed took it. "I'll be seeing you, Captain. Say goodbye to your men for me, huh?" Then, turning to Paul, Rourke said, "I'll have Sarah cook you the best meal in the world at the retreat. I'll see you there as soon as I can get them back."

"Sure, John—hey, John?"

Rourke turned and looked at the younger man.

"If something goes wrong, just—"

"It won't," Rourke said, smiling and snatching up his CAR-15. "It won't."

Chapter 43

It was dark, cold, raining still and the roads slick as Rourke turned off the highway and into the mountain passes. It had been a fool's play taking what had once been the Interstate, but the fastest route. He'd dodged a Russian roadblock perhaps seventy-five miles back, then taken to the Interstate again.

The farm where Sarah was staying was less than twenty miles ahead according to the map.

Rourke passed a farm house, a demolished sand-bag fence crumbling around it, the roof burnt off, and no signs of light or life in the rainy darkness.

He traveled on past dense woods, higher into the mountains, and saw a yellow light in the darkness. Rourke checked the map with the flickering blue-yellow flame of the Zippo, stopped and stared at the yellow light, lighting one of his small cigars and keeping the smoke cupped under his left hand as he stared past the darkness.

Sarah—he remembered the last time they had made love, just before he had gone to Canada just a few days before the night of the war. They had decided to try again. His passion, as she called it, for guns, for planning for disaster, for studying survivalism had been the undoing, she'd said so often, but she had been willing to try again, to see somehow if the two of them could resolve his planning for the inevitable with her yearning for peace. He remembered the look and smell of her dark hair, the gray-green eyes. He stared up at the starless sky, rain bathing his face. He remembered kissing her in the rain and how she tasted.

And there would be Michael, just six, but a man in so many ways already, the best of Sarah and the best of himself. And little Annie, four, small, beautiful, prone to too many tears and bizarre, but lovely laughter. Annie.

Rourke chewed down on the cigar butt, turned the bike toward the light and searched the trees for a path, found one and took the motorcycle across the field, the rain driving harder now.

Rourke stopped the jet-black Harley, kicked out the stand and dismounted, walking through the sloshing mud toward the small porch, the light—yellow and warm looking in the darkness—from a kitchen ceiling fixture. They apparently had a generator of their own, Rourke thought almost mechanically.

A dog barked, but not the howl of a wild one, and he stepped to the door and knocked. The door opened, the small porch flooded in the yellow light, and a red-haired boy in his mid-teens stood, his left arm in a sling and a pistol in his right hand.

"Relax, son," Rourke almost whispered, seeing the older woman behind him. More to the woman than the boy, Rourke said, "I'm John Rourke. Are you Mary?"

The woman nodded.

"My wife, Sarah—my boy, Michael—my daughter, Annie? I've come for them."

"Oh, my God," the woman said, tears welling up in her eyes and streaming down her cheeks.

Rourke said nothing.

"She was worried about you. I offered that she could stay, or at least leave the little boy and girl here after what she did for my sister's girl. I offered."

"Where are they?" Rourke whispered, staring down at the woman into the yellow light framing her just past the doorway, rain dripping from his face and hair, the light making him somehow lightheaded, around his eyes, and in his throat a tight feeling coming.

"She wouldn't—wanted to go look for you. Back into Georgia. She left this morning—"

"Horseback?" Rourke asked, his voice funny sounding.

"Yes—one for her, one for the boy and girl, and one for their things."

"Armed?" Rourke asked, the tight feeling growing in him.

"An AR-15 that somebody converted to full auto and a rubber-gripped .45 pistol," the red-haired boy said.

"Are they well? No one had been injured?" Rourke asked as though filling out a report.

"Fine—healthy—nothin' wrong with 'em I reckon," the woman stammered.

"Toward Georgia, you said," Rourke asked. "Any idea of the route?"

"I think she was gonna take the old highway that runs along the Interstate, you know it," the boy with the red hair said.

"Yes—thank you—and thank you, ma'am. We'll never forget your kindness. Should she come back before I find her—her and the children—keep her here. And you, son," Rourke said to the red-haired boy, his words hard now, "if she ever does, or you hear of where she is or where she's been, get the Resistance to contact Army Intelligence in Texas. Somehow."

"Yes, sir," the boy stammered, straightening his shoulders.

"Good night, ma'am," Rourke said to the woman named Mary.

Wringing her hands on the floral-print apron she wore, she whispered. "God bless you and let you find them."

"Yes, ma'am," Rourke said, forcing a smile, turning, walking down from the porch. He stopped by the Harley, the rain falling in sheets.

He was glad the woman hadn't asked him to stay. She'd known, he felt, that he wouldn't.

This morning—gone. Rourke sank to his knees in the mud beside the Harley, his lips drawn back, staring up at the lightless sky. "Why!" he shouted.

Rourke climbed up from his knees, realizing some

of the wetness on his face wasn't the rain, mounted the motorcycle, kicked up the stand, balanced the machine with his feet out of the mud ruts and throttled up as fast as he dared in the rutted field leading back toward the road.

He passed through the trees, turned back onto the country road, watched the rain in his single headlight, and gunned the Harley into the darkness, screaming, "Why!"

Preview of Survivalist 4:

THE DOOMSAYER

Rourke closed the Lowe Alpine Loco Pack and checked that it was secure on the back of the jet black Harley Davidson Low Rider. He scanned the ground in the early sunlight and checked that the fire was out and everything accounted for. He would need gasoline by the end of the day and was aiming toward one of the Strategic Reserve sites the new President of United States II, Samuel Chambers, had pinpointed for him weeks earlier. John Rourke had been out of the Retreat for nearly seven days, having re-equipped, waited a day while young Paul Rubenstein had prepared, then left the same day Paul had set out for Florida, Paul in quest of his parents to see if somehow they had survived the holocaust of the Night of The War—World War III. World War Last, he wondered, noting the haze around the sunrise, the redness of the atmosphere? The geiger counter strapped to the Harley still indicated normal radiation levels, but John Thomas Rourke was worried still.

In the seven days, there had been no sign of Sarah, his wife, nor Michael and Ann.

He snatched up his CAR-15, popped out the thirty-round magazine, worked the bolt and removed the chambered round there, then loaded the .223 solid into the magazine and snapped off the trigger, putting the magazine back up the well, bending his head as he slung the collapsible stock semi-automatic rifle across his back, muzzle down, scope covers in place.

He kicked away the stand on the Harley and started it, the humming of the engine somehow reassuring to him. He had chosen the Harley before the War because he had objectively felt it was the best—and it hadn't let him down. Like the Rolex Submariner on his wrist, the Colt rifle on his back, the Detonics pistols in the double shoulder rig under his brown leather jacket, the six-inch Colt Python on his right hip—and he had survived until now.

Rourke stared past the bike into the gorge below and the road climbing it from the river bottom.

Rourke revved the machine under him and started forward out of the small clearing where he had camped the night, following the mountains as long as he could before dropping to the Piedmont searching for some sign of his family—hoofprints perhaps, from the horses they had ridden as they had left Tennessee in search for him.

Rourke pushed the aviater sunglasses up against the bridge of his nose as he turned the bike from the clearing onto the winding animal trail leading out of the woods. He slowed the bike at the edge of the tree line, cutting it in a narrow arc and stopping, surveying the gorge, more clearly visible now below him, snapping up the leather jacket's collar against the cold—it was summer by the calendar. The oddity of the seasons worried him too.

He could hear the rushing water, but it was not that noise that caused him to cut the Harley's motor and listen, hardly daring to breath. A smile crossed his lips. Rourke lit one of his small, dark tobacco cigars in the blue yellow flame of the battered Zippo he carried and listened more intently, inhaling the grey smoke then exhaling it hard through his nostrils.

Gunfire, engine noises. The Brigands, Rourke thought, but below him along the road paralleling the gorge. He dismounted the bike, letting out the kick stand and walked toward the lip of ground looking down into the river bottom canyon. He snatched the Bushnell Armored 8x30s from the case on his right side under his jacket and focused them along the gorge road.

A single motorcycle, the rider low over the handlebars, and a hundred yards or less behind the rider were two dozen or so motorcycles, and behind them at a modest distance were a half dozen pickup trucks—men and women—Brigands—riding them. He focused in on the rider of the lead motorcycle. A woman, reddish brown hair riding on the slipstream behind her.

Rourke watched, the woman rounding a curve, the bike skidding from under her, out of control.

She pulled herself to her feet, the Brigands closing. They would want her for rape, for robbery and then for murder, Rourke knew. The girl had the bike up and was getting it going again, the Brigand pursuers less than thirty yards behind her now, gunfire again. As she righted the bike on the road below Rourke, he could see her twitch as a pistol shot echoed through the canyon, see her back arch, the bike weave, then see her lean low over the handlebars, lower than before. He focused in more tightly on her—her left hand looked to be streaming blood from some wound further up along her arm.

Rourke swept the binoculars back along the road,

the Brigand gang closing in on the woman, their weapons firing, some of them armed with sub-machineguns, men and women standing in the pickup truck beds speeding behind the Brigand bikers, firing rifles at the girl cyclist.

Rourke sighed, replacing the binoculars in their case, slipping the Colt CAR-15 from his back, the sling now on his right shoulder. He grasped the ears on the bolt and chambered the first round from the thirty-round magazine, then worked the safety to on.

Slowly, deliberately, he walked back to his own Harley, swung his right leg across and settled himself, then kicked away the stand. "Damnit," he rasped to himself, then gunned the Low Rider along the edge of the tree linej scanning the ground for a suitable access to the gorge below.

The path down into the gorge was steep and the gravel and rock and dirt slippery and loose beneath the Harley's wheels as Rourke balanced himself, his feet dragging the dirt as he headed his machine down into the gorge, the sound of the gunfire below him louder now, the face of the girl visible once as she'd looked up from the bike she rode, up and then back at the pursuing Brigand killers.

Something in the fleeting glimpse of the face had told him she was pretty.

Rourke hit the level of the gorge road, the Harley bouncing over a hummock of hard packed red clay and stone, the bike coming down hard, Rourke's jaw set against the impact, the wind of the slipstream as he accelerated the Harley blowing the hair from his forehead, his bike racing ahead to intercept the girl and put distance between himself and the nearest of the Brigand bikers, now less than a dozen yards behind him along the river road.

Rourke leaned low over his machine, throttling it out, the ripping and tearing sound of the exhaust from the laboriously worked-over engine reassuring in its strength, its very loudness. He was gaining on the girl, the girl low over her bike and at an awkward angle, gunshots echoing behind him from the Brigand bikers and the pickup trucks following them. Rourke swung the CAR-15 forward, thumbing off the safety, pointing the rifle behind him, firing it unseeing toward his pursuers. A little gunfire might slow them he thought—only a fool was eager to die.

Rourke swung the rifle back at his side, thumbing the safety on, letting the bike, the reddish brown-haired girl less than ten yards ahead of him now, the Japanese bike she rode seemingly at full throttle. There was a burst of gunfire—an automatic weapon Rourke determined, and he swerved his bike far left toward the edge of the road and the river bank. The girl ahead of him lurched—he could see the impact of the subgun slugs in the road, against the seat of the bike she rode, against her body, her body slumping low over her bike, the motorcycle weaving.

The road twisted ahead of him, Rourke throttling out the Harley in spite of it, closing the gap between himself and the wounded girl. Five yards, four, now six feet, fivew Three feet and then one.

NEL BESTSELLERS

SURVIVALIST 1: TOTAL WAR	*Jerry Ahern*	£1.50
SURVIVALIST 2: THE NIGHTMARE BEGINS	*Jerry Ahern*	£1.50
SURVIVALIST 4: THE DOOMSAYER	*Jerry Ahern*	£1.50
THE MOSCOW OPTION	*David Downing*	£1.25
DEVIL'S GUARD	*George Elford*	£1.95
KIZILKAR	*George Elford*	£1.50
I BOUGHT A STAR	*Thomas Firbank*	£0.90
WORLD WAR III	*Brian Harris*	£1.25
ASSAULT TROOP 1: BLOOD BEACH	*Ian Harding*	£1.50
ASSAULT TROOP 2: DEATH IN THE FOREST	*Ian Harding*	£1.50
ASSAULT TROOP 3: CLASH ON THE RHINE	*Ian Harding*	£1.60
LOS CHICOS DE LA GUERRA	*Daniel Kon*	£2.95
PQ17 CONVOY TO HELL	*Lund & Ludlam*	£0.75
THE WAR OF THE LANDING CRAFT	*Lund & Ludlam*	£0.80
JERSEY UNDER THE JACKBOOT	*R. C. F. Maugham, C.B.E.*	£0.95
DIEPPE: THE DAWN OF DECISION	*Jacques Mordal*	£1.75
GATEWAY TO HELL	*James Rouch*	£0.95
TIGER	*James Rouch*	£1.25
THE WAR MACHINES	*James Rouch*	£1.25
THE ZONE 1: HARD TARGET	*James Rouch*	£1.00
THE ZONE 2: BLIND FIRE	*James Rouch*	£1.00
THE ZONE 4: SKY STRIKE	*James Rouch*	£1.25
THE ZONE 5: OVERKILL	*James Rouch*	£1.25
THE LAST BATTLE	*Cornelius Ryan*	£2.95
THE LONGEST DAY	*Cornelius Ryan*	£1.95